About the author

Katerina Tsitoura was born and raised in Athens, Greece. She is a graduate of the School of Greek Language and Literature of the University of Athens, where she specialized in linguistics. She has attended various seminars on education, psychology, and creative writing. She has worked as an educator both in Greece and the United States of America. Currently, she is working as a copywriter and a teacher. She has had two books published in Greece by Gavriilides Publishing House.

THE CASTLE OF PERFECTION

KATERINA TSITOURA

THE CASTLE OF PERFECTION

Vanguard Press

VANGUARD PAPERBACK

© Copyright 2021
Katerina Tsitoura

The right of Katerina Tsitoura to be identified as author of this work has been asserted by her in accordance with the Copyright, Designs and Patents Act 1988.

All Rights Reserved

No reproduction, copy or transmission of this publication may be made without written permission.
No paragraph of this publication may be reproduced, copied or transmitted save with the written permission of the publisher, or in accordance with the provisions of the Copyright Act 1956 (as amended).

Any person who commits any unauthorised act in relation to this publication may be liable to criminal prosecution and civil claims for damages.

A CIP catalogue record for this title is available from the British Library.

ISBN 978 1 80016 182 5

*Vanguard Press is an imprint of
Pegasus Elliot MacKenzie Publishers Ltd.*
www.pegasuspublishers.com

First Published in 2021

**Vanguard Press
Sheraton House Castle Park
Cambridge England**

Printed & Bound in Great Britain

Dedication

Dedicated to my mother, Pat Kraras-Tsitoura, who is also the translator of the book.

Acknowledgements

Special thanks to my supportive partner, Konstadinos Theodorou.

Special thanks to my mother and translator of the book, Pat Kraras.

Special thanks to my loving friends Dimitra Michael, Nicolas Karaliotas, Alex Aggelakis, Stratos Karamichalakis, and Thanasis Sklavos.

Special thanks to Mr Sammy Gavriilides, the man who believed in me and encouraged me to pursue my dreams.

ONE

Do not keep this fairy tale to yourself. It goes a long way back in time and recounts a story that, for all you know, may be true. But it calls for something on your part. Indeed, it does call for something. It calls for you to feel it. And then to share it. To change. And then to change the others. Meanwhile, the hands of the clock turn, the night falls bleak, and dawn, like a choosy hostess, welcomes only those who are discerning enough to see the light. I am rambling on, and I may be tiring you. I have so much to tell you, however, about faraway lands that may never have existed and about events so distressing that you have to close your eyes and pretend they never really happened.

Well, once upon a time, in some corner of the world, the perfect ones of this esteemed humanity had begun to get alarmingly exasperated. You see, it is not a small matter to parade your impeccable style, your refined manners, and your indisputable talent in places that are filled with gaudy lighting and run-of-the-mill table companions. One day, the most perfect one of them all, the famous Judge Compulsion came to the crucial decision that it was time to convene an urgent meeting regarding this matter.

The time of the meeting was arranged for seven o'clock in the evening, shortly after the setting of the sun when the day takes its leave from the sky and mysteries are worked out much more effectively with a flashlight in hand. The thunder was wounding the recently blue sky while the raindrops were soaking the well-ironed shirts and the perfect curls.

Judge Compulsion swaggered in, slightly tightened his permanently crooked mouth, and stood in front of the microphone.

'Ladies and gentlemen, friends, you are here. The stars will soon make their appearance, but our brightness will permanently fade if we confine ourselves to narrow streets and simple-minded people. I dare us all, therefore, to the ultimate challenge. Let us create our own society, a society of excellence, a society that has no precedence. Let us construct the most imposing castle, the Castle of Perfection. In our midst, we will make sure to have fabulous riches, unsurpassed minds, masterpiece writers, and the finest melodies. Do we actually need the mediocre, commonplace, run-of-the-mill masses? This question, I am certain, will prevail upon any qualms you may have regarding the course of action I am recommending.'

A great roar came as an answer from the crowd. Judge Compulsion smiled smugly but quickly puckered his lips austerely. He then looked left and right to make sure that no one had caught sight of his momentarily light disposition.

On the way back, the perfect ones walked with their heads down as if they were seeking the Earth's approval for their betrayal. However, it was the middle of a heavy winter, and nature, stripped of crops and fruit, seemed to be in mourning for its losses.

The resourceful salesman was the first to break the awkward silence of his fellow travelers. 'Come on! It is no great secret that they are incapable of properly advertising even simple sports shoes.'

'Having to teach lazy people bores me to death,' added the highly educated teacher gloomily.

'Simple arithmetic is a better fit for the ignorant ones,' the exemplary accountant burst out.

'And if you, my dear lady, waste your time with crossword puzzles, why must I consider you a colleague?' the super-organized secretary complained.

Then all of them, in one voice but with no soul, agreed that it was time for change. They would have to leave year-long relationships behind, but the glorious future would compensate them for their sacrifices.

The very next morning, preparations began. They took place at an amazingly fast pace while the horses were running frantically at the racetrack of ambition. Soon, the day came when the horses reached the finish line, and the bettors waited in line to collect their winnings.

A lot of people assembled at the port of the city. Some were holding tissues to wipe away their tears, while others were using their cameras to capture the historic departure and hold on to it for eternity. Tears, smiles, sun, clouds. The fate of mortals: to welcome and to bid farewell; to come to life and then to depart. The final hugs were given, the promises to keep in touch—some superficial and hurried, others profound and honest—were exchanged, and the ship sailed.

Seconds after its departure and right before the ship moved on to the vastness of the ocean and the page turned forever, a loud and clear voice was heard above the crying. A youth with wild brown curls, striking black eyes, and colorful clothes temporarily put a stop to the maiden voyage.

'Now hold on a minute

and to the Castle take me too.

You are far too prudent,

and the moment slips away,' he recited pompously.

Judge Compulsion—who hated anything and everything that got in the way of his austere program—sneered with his permanently crooked mouth and, turning to the experienced and competent captain, said, 'Hell! Do not let go of the steering wheel just because of this crazy man. Continue. This is an order!'

However, the outstanding magician, who was also considered a seer, suddenly interfered.

'The magic ball foresees it clearly:

Without the crazy one,

the New World will not proceed.'

Judge Compulsion chewed a piece of his bow tie for a few seconds and, fearing all superstitions, grudgingly gave his consent.

The unexpected fellow traveler boarded the ship with a dance number, bowed theatrically to the audience, and thanked the perfect ones profusely.

'There is an empty cabin at the end of the corridor. Number 20, if my memory does not deceive me. You can get settled in there. A long journey is awaiting us, and you will need some rest,' the judge dryly informed the crazy one.

The crazy one moved down the corridor, whistling a tune cheerfully.

The ship finally left the port, and the familiar figures slowly faded away.

As soon as the sun turned orange, the perfect ones assembled in the luxurious lounge of the ship to enjoy their dinner. They sat in their gold armchairs and enthusiastically welcomed the glittering china with the culinary pleasures that they contained. While they were enjoying their delicious meal, they would often put their forks down either to straighten their expensive clothes or to boast about their accomplishments.

Just before dinner was over, the crazy youth appeared. He placed his straw chair in the middle of the lounge and clumsily scratched his guitar.

'For the life of me, I can't remember your name,' the famous surgeon said.

'Names are borrowed labels,

but call me Cheron, if you must,' the youth answered.

'Do you always talk as if you are singing?' the distinguished architect wondered.

'I am just whistling a tune

that leads to the treasures of truth.'

'Oh, yes, of course! The cobbler! What kind of work is that, my dear, to constantly loosen our beautiful shoes?' the surgeon retorted.

'You balance on very high shoes

and thus fail to breathe properly.'

'Please, my dear young man! How can I forget that you are to blame for my stumbling in my top performance? Tighter, I had told you. Tighter! Even the pumps of the biggest female basketball player would have served my performance better than your shoes. But, let me not think about that day because it upsets me so very much,' broke in the accomplished ballet dancer.

'I can just see you before me that night

swaying sensually and light.'

'So sensually that it was a miracle I was not jeered by the audience. My pumps were hurled in the direction of the judges, twice. In fact, they caught one of them in the eye. He had his good luck to thank for not being seriously injured.'

'Enough.' Judge Compulsion sighed, exhausted. 'You have all heard the wizard. Cheron is now a member of our unique society. The most unfitting member? Possibly. Nevertheless, we have no choice but to welcome him into our midst.'

'And to find a different profession for him to practice,' added the surgeon.

'Or at least, buy some insoles for our shoes,' the ballet dancer remarked.

The ship kept fading deeper and deeper into the vast ocean while the countless stars led the steering wheel to the unknown and exciting, to the faraway and elusive, to the most imposing building, to the most golden palace ever: The Castle of Perfection.

TWO

Five years later

'My God! Time just flies by us!' the eminent lawyer concluded profoundly as he straightened his black tie.

'Time, my friend, an hourglass governs our lives; we are all walking on a tightrope. Below us the abyss, and behind us the memories. Good or bad, they always define us. And we just move on, no matter what. Just like nimble acrobats, we balance between celebrations and mournings, begging that the rope not break. Could it be that we are the ones gnawing at it?' the first-rate photographer wondered.

'We do our very best. Do not forget that our generation is making history. Do not forget the heritage we are passing on to our descendants.'

'Right. The Castle of Perfection. The greatest proof that, even if we sprinkle silver on the rope, the acrobat will continue to be terrified of the abyss below him.'

'Do the perfect ones get terrified?'

'Oh, even more so than the others. Essence just slips through their porcelain fingers while the merciless darkness rings the alarm of their mortal nature,' the capturer of beautiful moments ascertained.

'Do you have any regrets?' mumbled the lawyer.

'About our having shut ourselves up in here, you mean?'

'You make it sound as if we are in prison.'

'Aren't we?'

'We have sacrificed a lot. No one can deny that,' admitted the lawyer sadly.

'Partners, children, friends.'

'You always lose something, my dear.'

'But to gain what?'

'Immortality,' the lawyer replied halfheartedly.

'The confirmation of narcissism, you mean. Food for the arrogant ego and two broken wings. This is what we will take with us to the abyss.'

'What about your work?' Don't you just savor the sacred moments of creativity? Those unique, magical moments when the universe bows to your lenses?'

'I have ceased to enjoy my work,' the photographer answered dryly.

'Nevertheless, you have made a name for yourself throughout the world,' the lawyer assured him.

'Perfection has become a punishment for me. For some time now, all I capture in my pictures are expressionless faces. An empty box with impeccable wrapping; this is what I offer my people. In the kaleidoscope of nature, in the caresses and the slashes, in the skyscrapers and the basements, in the sunshine and the storms, in everything, the truth that we have stifled screams out. I want you to remember this.'

'Is there a way out of this?' the legal expert inquired.

'Is there?'

'The contract clearly stipulates that, if someone violates the oath of perfection, he is immediately expelled from our society.'

'You are naïve. A mind manipulation keeps us prisoners in the Castle. We will never manage to escape.'

'You speak as if it is an addiction,' the lawyer pointed out.

'It is undoubtedly an addiction. You know, only one person here arouses my interest. However, it is explicitly forbidden for us to associate with him.'

'Cheron… what an oddball!'

'He is authentic. In our society, we have gotten to the point of confusing spontaneity with madness and despondency with maturity.'

'Let's go.' The lawyer terminated the discussion abruptly.

'Is it nine o'clock?' the photographer wondered, looking at his watch.

'Yes. The general assembly begins in a few minutes, and you are well aware of how much our king resents tardiness. Have you got your lens?'

'I always carry it with me and turn it into fancy bows that console the empty boxes.'

THREE

Judge Compulsion looked carefully around the room and was intoxicated by the obedient gazes of the multitude. You see, he craved to feel awe in the souls of the people under his power.

'Respect walks hand in hand with fear,' he would often be heard saying.

This crowd was, in fact, his army, a squadron of excellent human beings that conquered the world on his behalf.

His mind frequently wandered back to his parents. 'We live for a forehead without wrinkles and a life without mistakes,' they would reiterate.

Now, as far as his forehead was concerned, he did succeed in keeping the wrinkles away—with the kind contribution of the matchless plastic surgeon, of course. However, he was still struggling with the ghost of imperfection and his permanently crooked mouth.

'If no light enters the soul,

do not in all seriousness expect

the mouth to actually straighten up,' the cobbler sang from time to time.

Oh, how he hated the cobbler! He walked as if he were performing a dance number, and he laughed heartily, even with his eyes. The judge put up with him, however, because he feared jinxes, and the magician-seer had made a crystal-clear prediction. So be it. An oddball like Cheron could not really destroy their high-gear society. This is what Compulsion believed, or at least hoped.

The impartial king stood before the microphone. The once bashful child now basked in the omnipotent version of himself, and this revenge was accompanied by a sweet feeling. The hoarse voice of the monarch over the microphone immediately captivated the attention of the audience.

'Ladies and gentlemen, I will not waste your time. For all those of you in here who are seeking a lifeboat to gain entrance into our ship, the news is delightful. The procedure is formally underway. For the sake of history. For the sake of all those pages that are craving for our ink and for all those books that will render us immortal. Our first station is the Castle of the Divergent. You can count on one thing for certain: perfection is the only acceptable divergence. Perfection is what we worship, and it is the only divergence worthy of the throne. No one and nothing else, qualifies to be called divergent. Dangerous? Definitely! They attack the norm just like unruly pirates and dismantle law and order. We intend to bend their resistance and bring the apples of their eyes to the palace. In essence, we will save the cream of the crop. They, in turn, will reward us with blind obedience. A transaction. Everything is a transaction. We endorse only the outstanding ones. Tomorrow, I am setting off with my team for the place where one can hear only digestible songs and insipid philosophizing. May the winds be favorable in our lofty mission.'

Loud applause, bright flashes, impressive ribbons. Empty boxes. There was also a tune coming from the back of the huge room.

'Do not for a moment undermine the divergent,
and at all times, love the genuine.
The genuine will, indeed, rescue freedom
and liberate you from your burdens.'

Some comprehended the tune and secretly danced to it in their rooms with pictures of loved ones around them and with tears that refused to dry up. Then, they double-locked their chest of memories, dusted their awards meticulously, and pretended that the above tune had never come out of the lips of that oddball.

'Damn you, Cheron!' the judge mumbled, annoyed, while his imperial throne was rocking nervously and the bashful boy from the past was still nesting inside him.

FOUR

The outstanding judge, Mr. Compulsion, and his unmatched staff are organizing the most ambitious undertaking. All those who are paralyzed by the dreary mediocrity around them will finally attain their rightful place in the Castle. A dream is coming true for the worthy ones, and the Earth is being transformed, laying claim to golden awards.

The man dropped the newspaper onto his desk, took another sip of coffee, and let out a dejected sigh.

The man was Mr. Compassionate, and the fact is that he knew Judge Compulsion all too well. How could it be otherwise? They grew up in the same family and were, consequently, considered siblings. That is if, in your mind, family relations involve not soul connection but rather ova and sperm that passionately—or even halfheartedly—come together.

You know—and I count on your discretion—at one time, the omnipotent judge was a sickly and terribly introverted boy. He would shut himself up in his room for days on end and hide in desperation behind his books. The world seemed inhospitable to him as his classmates derided him for his timidity, and his own parents, Mr. and Mrs. Flawless, were judgmental even regarding his breathing patterns.

Mr. and Mrs. Flawless, on the other hand, enjoyed the respect that everyone showed them and basked in their inestimable riches. Both plastic surgeons, they belonged to that category of people who wear masks and remove consciences. Everyone from all around the world sought their dexterous scalpels for the purpose of acquiring French noses, nicely shaped lips, wrinkle-free maturity and, generally, appearances without any blemishes.

I am rambling on again, however, and the hourglass is signaling to me impatiently. Mr. and Mrs. Flawless— let me continue—raised their children with strict rules and the proper beauty standards. They weighed both of them on a regular basis, they counted their freckles and pimples, and they even subjected them to the 'necessary' surgery. No, nothing extreme. I am talking about minor nose and ear correction surgery. Now, my friend, you are surely wondering why Mr. Compulsion never had his mouth corrected. This is, indeed, quite a mystery, I must say. You may not believe what I am about to tell you, and I don't blame you in the least. But it did happen exactly this way. The Flawless couple repeatedly performed surgery to correct this defect that their son had, but—oddly enough—their son's mouth would become crooked again within a few months. The famous plastic surgeons put their scalpels aside, sighed in frustration, and finally gave up.

One family, two brothers, two completely different life histories, both involving a struggle with golden cages and the keys to these cages.

When Mr. Compassion turned eighteen, he went on a sacred mission. He traveled a great deal and, on his travels, he came in contact with both wealthy people and those who lived on the streets. He sang spellbinding tunes with traveling performers and saw the magic of life in humble huts where they tricked their hunger by gazing, mesmerized, at ocean waters. He eventually understood how things stood. This world had no room for desperate poets, incorrigibly romantic dreamers, child-like souls, and authentic, spontaneous laughter.

The margin and the mainstream constantly lock horns with each other, unstitch and stitch again because the thread gets tangled up and does not allow for freedom to be left as a gift under the Christmas tree. The Castle of the Divergent was then established, and it soon bloomed like a spring garden. In its midst, you could find children who did not have parents, street performers, homeless artists, and scientists who were short on both resources and narcissism.

From his window, Mr. Compassion was now watching the children chasing each other lightheartedly in the schoolyard and the charming 'crazy' ones whistling melodies about suns, hopes, and sleeping beauties that finally wake up.

At that point, he took an oath: 'This castle will not be touched by the hand of Compulsion. This rainbow will always shine brightly in its place. It will always be lighting up cloudy skies and frightened hearts. It will never cease to dance with spring, even in the middle of a heavy winter.'

FIVE

The end of the school year. Games and hearty laughter. Cheerfulness and hide-and-seek. Hide-and-seek from friends as well as from the changing seasons, which threaten youth and innocence and run much faster than the school children themselves.

Beside the fountain, a group of children started chatting.

'Cynic! I can't help but wonder how you chose such a name,' gasped a juicy little girl with a round, cute face.

'A cynic, my friend, does not swallow the fairy tales without chewing them first, so no one can fool him. A cynic wonders, questions, doubts.' The boy with the brown hair and jovial face was quick to answer.

'You contaminate joy with shadows and see clouds in places where there is only sunshine.'

'I just do not lose sight of the fact that the rays of the sun can burn us once in a while,' he said in an attempt to disarm her.

'You are just too cynical.'

'Actually, we are saying the same thing, my dear Optimist. If you are asking me, your mission sounds somewhat dangerous. You are hovering around in a world of your own, but one day you are bound to land on the ground without a parachute. I just hope I will be nearby to save you from the worst.'

'But optimism does not really involve broken wings that you wear and lose height. Optimism is more about our refusal to abandon the plans that our hearts are set on executing, I would say.'

'What if these plans flirt with the unfeasible? Why don't we then leave them in peace?'

'Because they offer us the opportunity to live. Away from our comfort zone, the elusive seems like just a dream that we never really pursued. You see, we are at all times both the pilots and the terrorists of our flight,' Optimist insisted.

'How about you? How did you end up with the honor of being called Quirky?' Cynic changed the direction of the conversation, turning to the blonde girl with the huge, blue eyes who was trying hard to keep her balance on one leg.

'Actually, it is not that difficult to figure out. I throw my things all over the place, and I go for long walks in my own universe.'

'No one can dispute that you have changed ten schoolbags in just a few months,' the boy confirmed.

'Phew! That is exactly where the meaning of applying yourself lies. We need to rise above the comfort or the pain that our label represents,' Optimist broke in.

'Then, why are you constantly raising objections to what I say? I made it my mission to get rid of the "realistic attitude to life."' Her classmate defended himself humorously.

'But you choose exactly the same nickname every single summer. No originality. You don't learn your lessons, and so you fail to make progress. It is as if you stay back in the same class every year,' the girl insisted.

'Guys, I chose Reserved as my name.' A boy with a low voice, curly hair, huge glasses, and kind eyes timidly entered the conversation.

'Oh! Of course! You have finally come to your senses and decided to harness your exuberant nature.' Cynic teased him.

Quirky nervously broke in. 'They are coming tomorrow. I wonder what will happen.'

'Whatever fate has in store for us. The best thing for everyone.' Optimist assured her, holding her hand tightly.

'We may have to part with each other. Quirky paints superbly. Obviously, they will take her with them. And you, Optimist, withdraw to your laboratory for hours and conduct innovative experiments. Unfortunately, the situation has gone out of our director's hands,' Reserved commented sadly.

'There is always hope,' the girl with the never-ending positive thinking interjected.

'Actually, the pumpkin is the only one that managed to make its grand appearance as a carriage.

We, without a fairy godmother on our side, will have difficulty being saved,' Cynic argued.

Quirky burst out in tears. 'They will imprison me in the Castle of Perfection. I've known this since yesterday. The announcement came with the characteristic miniature of the Castle that is sent to all the ostensibly lucky ones.'

'That won't happen.' Optimist comforted her, giving her a gentle hug.

'The Castle of the Divergent will be dismantled, and we will be scattered to the four corners of the horizon. Let's take our measures, leaving aside any illusions we may have. At least, this is what I recommend. Quirky, do you have the miniature with you?' Cynic wanted to know.

'I believe I squeezed it into my pocket,' she answered and fumbled around nervously in the pocket of her jeans. 'Yes, here it is.'

'Splendid! In ten minutes, let's all meet in Optimist's laboratory. No one ever goes there. We will have our privacy.'

The laboratory was at the end of the right wing of the building. The four friends hurriedly entered it and double-locked the door. Cynic addressed the others.

'Listen carefully, please. Here, we have become each other's family, the family that we have been deprived of. If our fate is good to us, we will meet again. Under different circumstances, of course. Older and different in appearance. I propose that we form a map of recognition and reunion by breaking the miniature into four pieces. Quirky, make sure you don't lose your piece. On its own, the miniature has little value but, if we manage to eventually join the pieces, I will truly believe in miracles.'

The childhood friends shook hands and took an oath that was probably far too big a load for their small shoulders.

'To the broken pieces that will reunite our souls,' they all shouted out.

The time was passing. Thick darkness brought a night that seemed to last longer than usual. The sun had qualms about rising, fearing that its first rays would mark the end of first true love.

SIX

In the morning, heavy rain rocked the sky and made a point of enshrouding the summer in darkness. Mr. Compassion had been expecting this day for quite some time. He had already made his decisions. He would definitely not give his consent to the enlistment of the select ones—at whatever cost.

He suddenly brought to mind a very strange man he had met decades before on his trip to Europe. The strange man was dressed in rags, and he seemed to be obsessed with taming his thick mustache. He kept staring outside the train window as if he wished to escape from his own fate. At times, tears would come to his eyes. He dried them hurriedly with a tissue, and then his hand would automatically seek his mustache again as if it were the last steady thing in his otherwise broken-up life.

Compassion had been watching him for some time before nudging him gently on the shoulder.

'Are you feeling well, sir?'

'You know, I have not, in the past, been the same man you see traveling next to you today. The fact is that we never wake up as the same person we were on the previous day, and the days that follow also hold in store so many changes for our fate. If my gray hair has taught me anything, it is that both despair and joy have the same cost. Sorrows break us up into many pieces but, with strong glue, we manage to become wiser. And then there are joys and triumphs—sneaky comrades, my young friend. They shower us with the illusion of supremacy and give us a ticket to a train that runs at breakneck speed. We superficially go by train stations. We also superficially overtake other travelers and hope that, at the end of the race, these fellow travelers of our arrogant coaches will heal the wounds from the fall. I have come to the conclusion that joys require a lot more strength,' the man said and kept his silence after that.

Barricaded in his office, the director of the Castle of the Divergent could now feel the impending change in his own fate as the steps of the perfect ones, almost deafening, came closer and closer.

The door of the office broke down with a decisive blow, and the honorable judge appeared, accompanied by three of his perfect bodyguards. The two brothers met once again. The distance that separated them was now greater than ever. For a minute, they exchanged glances—glances that indicated their past history so much more swiftly than words could ever describe it.

'Will you cooperate?' Compulsion asked sharply.

'You are breaking apart a family just to satisfy your arrogant whim,' Compassion said, trying to bring his brother to his senses.

'You call it an "arrogant whim," I call it a sublime mission. I believe it is a matter of perspective. Do you remember what you kept repeating to me over and over again? "Do not be afraid of the others' insults. We look at the world with our own eyes, and there are as many truths as there are ways of looking at things." The time has come for you to rejoice. I am no longer afraid,' the most perfect of the perfect announced dryly.

'And, yet, you are timidly curling up at the top of the mountain.'

'You are talking nonsense. The modern-day messiahs are the only ones who manage to set foot on the mountaintops.'

'The same frail child is still hiding behind the honorary titles.'

'Your psychoanalysis is tiring me. The Castle of the Divergent is becoming an obstacle to my plans. I will take the perfect ones of this castle along with me. The rest can go on in their mediocre way through life. I could not care less about them,' the judge insisted.

'I will not allow it!' Compassion shouted.

However, just as he was finishing his sentence, the handcuffs turned him into a prisoner and, consequently, trapped the people's hopes in golden cages once again.

The conscription had begun. The gates opened, the mediocre ones were turned away, and a glittering carriage welcomed the fresh batch of perfect people. Quirky saw her friends fading on the horizon. Tears were coming down her cheeks. She sought the miniature piece in her jeans pocket. 'As long as this piece exists, fairy godmothers cannot be done away with,' she consoled herself.

SEVEN

Fifteen years later

The famous artist peered at her figure in the mirror. Today it was her birthday; she was turning twenty-seven. Fifteen years earlier, on this exact day, a sudden turn of events had marred her destiny. Ever since that day, she hated birthdays, left the birthday cakes in the refrigerator, and entertained thoughts of wishing the Castle of Perfection would go up in flames when she finally did get around to blowing out the candles on her cake.

'Don't cry. Sadness is not considered proper fuel for your glittering carriage,' the people around her would tell her again and again.

Growing up in the hands of the venerable judge was a truly unique experience. Surly as he was, he had excluded any kind of romance early on in his life. He did, of course, do some dancing with a number of dates; however, he never synchronized his awkward steps to theirs and, as a result, his bed remained empty of company on the nights when the moon sought stars. Even so, he had always longed for a child, not because he had ample tenderness to offer them but rather because he wanted them to carry on his legacy. At some point, Compulsion carefully studied all the prospects at hand and came to the conclusion that girls prove to be somewhat more loyal and respectful to parents than boys. He then went on to make a safe investment. The artist had a stable hand and a splendid imagination. The magnificent portrait of her father would grace all the paintings of the future. The particular adoption would, thus, bring him immortality. An honorable transaction—don't you agree?

The adopted daughter and the cold father never managed to build a meaningful relationship. He, austere and taciturn, had difficulty communicating with the girl, a creature that was very often lost in dreams and colors. The prohibitions were countless, and the walls were painted gray. As time passed, the young woman saw her career soar and her psychological state plummet. In fact, the leading psychotherapist diagnosed her with 'panic attacks' a couple of winters earlier.

'It happens even to the best among us, my dear, or should I say especially to the best ones. Anxiety and the constant quest for perfection exhaust us. We are engines, so sometimes we run out of fuel. I recommend rest and tranquility, my dear girl,' he advised her with paternal tenderness.

The famous painter felt temporarily relieved when she understood that at least she was not having a heart attack. Of course—to be absolutely frank with you—her symptoms never completely disappeared. When she held her brushes, the heavy weight did seem to leave her chest, but it always came back and haunted her. Also, creativity was encumbered by the austere materials and suffocated under the strict directives.

The king of the Castle made it quite clear to her from the very beginning: 'You will be given specific topics, and you will follow our instructions with unrivaled professionalism. Social concerns prove to be the bad habit of lazy people. Avoid the subjects of poverty and misery. Aim at luxury, architectural masterpieces, beautiful shapes, and symmetrical faces. The talented ones and the mediocre ones, the fortunate ones, and the outcasts. We never become equals. We are eternally divided into camps. Therefore, you need to choose your allies with prudence and wisdom. Your allies must be the worthy ones who will ensure you of success and triumph.'

The young woman had gotten the message. The brushes were handcuffed while the miserable paintings fumbled for keys in the darkness of the golden palace and the tight pockets of the glittering suits.

The perfect ones, completely preoccupied with the race for first place, seldom had the time or the disposition for chatting. The artist gradually shut herself off from the rest but did meet the cobbler once in a while and, at those times, she had the feeling that the fairy godmother was secretly smiling at her again from the forgotten corners of the palace.

She often brought to mind her first meeting with the eccentric Castle resident.

'Put on these shoes, I beg of you,

and do tell me whether they offer you a proper walk,' he had sung to her.

She had eagerly put the shoes on and loved them so much that she was spinning around gracefully.

'Finally! My size! Could you please explain to me why everyone here chooses such tight shoes?' she had asked Cheron.

'When this detail is perceived,

there is always hope to be redeemed,' he replied.

'Redeemed.' She held on to this word like a good luck charm. Redemption, freedom, as well as a friend who is different, unconventional, full of life!

Needless to say, the judge did not approve of his daughter's friendship with the cobbler. Nonetheless, the two of them were set on wrinkling masks and loosening shoes, on coloring brushes and brightening up paintings.

EIGHT

Lunchtime was set at one o'clock on the dot. Not a minute earlier, not a minute later. The young artist remembered this rule well, just as she always remembered her very first lunch with her new family.

She had arrived ten minutes late at that first lunch. In the spacious kitchen, the silverware and the chinaware seemed to be suffocating from the cleanliness while she could swear that she was able to clearly see her reflection in the waxed wooden floor.

Judge Compulsion was already seated at the head of the table. His permanently crooked mouth became even more crooked as soon as he saw the girl. Then he coughed dryly. Even his cough sounded austere. The round clock, fixed on the wall exactly across from his seat, kept count of every moment and did not forgive lack of punctuality.

'You are late,' he snapped at her.

That was it. Since then, both of them were unfailingly at their seats and ready for lunch at exactly one o'clock.

They really did not have much to say to each other. They usually ate in silence. On this particular day, however, the judge seemed eager to communicate something to his daughter.

'There are only a few weeks left until the international art exhibition. What will you prepare for it?'

'Oh… my brush seems to have run out of ideas lately,' the artist replied halfheartedly.

'I see. You do realize, of course, that it is not enough for you to participate in the contest with something that is just fine and decent. You should be aiming at the lofty and the unrivaled. Do not just sit there and wait for inspiration to join you. Seek it out yourself and demand that it led you to perfection,' he advised her.

The young woman kept silent for a while.

'Perfection… naturally. This is what we always strive for,' she agreed with a faintly ironic tone in her voice.

'We blindly serve perfection. We worship it, and it worships us. It is a mutually beneficial transaction,' Compulsion noted.

'I can't help but wonder how this transaction benefits us. The apprehension of the top psychoanalyst must have reached your ears.'

'I suppose you are talking about the panic attacks.'

'Yes. They are spreading in the Castle like an epidemic. Strange, don't you think?'

'My dear, you are still very young, and you don't know much about life. I will not deny the fact that the symptoms are annoying, to say the least. The knot in the throat, the difficulty in breathing, the trembling of the hands. Awful. I, myself, have had firsthand experience with these symptoms, and the truth is that they still pay me a visit once in a while,' the judge admitted.

'So, to what do you attribute them?'

'Our mission is a difficult one. We gradually discard our human nature and turn into deities. The height does cause dizziness but we, using our talent as Dramamine, will ignore the symptoms and soar to the heaven of our myth.'

'What if nature is ringing an alarm to warn us of our being guilty of hubris? I often hear the cobbler singing the same tune over and over again:

"Your flaws do not exterminate,

if in profuse light you wish to remain.

The heart will surely make mistakes,

if the truth it wishes to locate."'

Judge Compulsion sighed, perturbed.

'The cobbler... an oddball that you choose to consider reliable. He cannot even mend our shoes properly. All he does is reap the fruits of our hard work.'

'Then, how did a contemptible man like him end up in the Castle of Perfection?'

'How did your dear friend explain it?' the judge inquired.

'Nothing is ever done by chance.

Everything will come to light

before the final curtain falls.'

'Let us just say then that it is our destiny to put up with his reasoning—and his loose shoes, of course.'

The stepdaughter disagreed. 'But the shoes he brings are indeed in our size.'

Compulsion lost his temper.

'Enough with your joke. Everyone in the Castle is complaining about him, and you insist on being the devil's advocate. He is such a good-for-nothing that it is impossible for us to find a more worthwhile job for him to do. So we clench our teeth and put up with him. I am held back from taking action on this by the seer's prophecy; otherwise, he would be rotting in prison along with your favorite director.'

'So many years have gone by. Why don't you show compassion and just let the director go?' the girl unexpectedly protested.

'Young lady, you have overstepped your limits. At my side, you have been given a luxurious home, an excellent education, and exceptional prospects. Don't you harbor any feelings of gratitude for your benefactor?' he shouted.

'I had a house. You destroyed it. I had a family. I haven't seen them since you brought me here. You have given me a lot of things, but they are inanimate, just like you. Your gold fabrics have deprived me of embraces, and your sharp commands have maimed true love forever.'

Compulsion started chewing a piece of his bow tie.

'I will not shut you up in the dungeon yet. I have always admired talent, and your talent is even more enormous than your ingratitude. However, you fail to abide by our rules. You are constantly protesting as if the revolution has become your second nature. Let us cut off this conversation here and now before we are forced to reconsider our relationship. Go to your studio immediately and come up with your best work ever,' the honorable judge ordered her angrily.

Then he hurriedly left the table and withdrew into his gray bedroom.

NINE

Thirty days. That was exactly the number of days left until the international art exhibition took place. In thirty days, the mediocre ones would, once again, come into contact with the outstanding ones. Once a year. That is what the great judge had decided. Every year on this day, the parents meet their children, old lovers exchange quick caresses, and friends fall into each other's arms. Briefly. As briefly as the dreams last on the nights that stars fall from the sky. Then everyone wakes up. They pick up the stars from the ground and lay them on the porches of their humdrum life, the humdrum life that, on the one hand, keeps them apart but, on the other hand, binds them together through memories.

The artist always looked forward to these exhibitions. However, no one from her past life ever showed up at the Castle.

Thirty days. Thirty days but the brushes remained in their place. In front of her, a blank canvas. If this canvas could speak, it would beg for colorful smudges and bumbling lines. Traditionally, a canvas has never been a fan of neatness and order. Such conditions do not agree with it. A canvas, as a rule, craves for life and disorderly imagination.

The brilliant artist felt her eyes watering and the annoying knot tightening her throat as if it were flirting with her last breath. A dead end. No way out was in sight.

At that very point, she heard a knock on the door.

'Come in,' she said dryly.

A man came in and took a deep bow.

'Cheron! You have no idea how happy I am to see you!' she said, falling into his arms.

'Tears running down your cheeks,

and sharp gasps coming from your throat

do threaten your serenity and peace.'

'They are demanding that I come up with a masterpiece, but my hand will no longer comply with their orders. Soon, when I am imprisoned in a cell, I will surely regret my inertia.'

'What is a prison, in truth?

Is it the dungeon and the cell?

Or is it actually our golden cage?'

'I understand what you mean. I have always considered myself a prisoner in the Castle. The people here have nothing in common with me, and I certainly have nothing in common with them. Nonetheless, you know very well how things are down there. Every day at lunchtime, you are the one who carries a few scraps of food to the director, and he, dressed in rags, is simply awaiting his death.'

'I have sung this to you plenty of times;

the sharp turns always end up somewhere,' he said, gently touching her.

'They do end up somewhere. All experiences teach us something. They make us better people. More enlightened. Dead ends do open up roads. I am struggling to believe you, but life seems so unfair! And then there is the problem of hope. It keeps getting farther and farther away. I have no courage to run and catch up with it before it completely fades away.'

'Do not run,

stay still a while

and to your soul

listen with all your might.'

'If I could do that! If only I would dare to do that. My brushes would catch fire and soon finish my best work.' She sighed, disheartened.

'You have to walk onto the fire

if you are to tame the monsters,' he challenged her.

'Yet, the monsters become executioners and demand that I be silent if I wish not to disappear.'

'The time has come

for you to break the rules,

and your own train catch on time,' her friend urged her.

'You are advising me to bypass… the prohibitions… at whatever cost…'

'There is no greater cost

than fear's fake signal.

Disregard the fear,

and the whole world conquer,' he insisted.

The young woman fully understood. The time had come. Exactly thirty days. She would buckle down and do what she had to do. She was late—fifteen years overdue. The knot in the throat disappeared. The brush moved with enthusiasm. The lines were dancing, and rhythm adorned their notes with beautiful colors. Outside the window, she saw the figures of all her loved ones coming to life and smiling at her. It seemed as if they were whispering to her that happiness requires bravery and freedom needs assertiveness.

TEN

Mr. Compulsion took a good look at his blue suit and straightened his red tie. Then he carefully checked his hair. The world-class hairdresser's natural dye had done wonders for it. It seemed that time was not capable of spoiling his perfection. It did chase him, but he constantly conjured up new and imaginative hiding places.

The gates would be opened up in one hour. Everything was ready. A swarm of wretches—the unfortunate, mediocre wretches—would soon be spilling into the Castle of Perfection. It was common knowledge that the judge did not think highly of his guests. In fact, he could not care less about their fate.

On this day, however, he would often bring to mind the emotionally charged meeting of the ideal professionals many years back. They had all assembled in the conference room with crumpled hearts and neatly folded pictures.

'We really miss our loved ones.'

'Time passes far too slowly without their warm presence.'

One after the other would shout out.

It was at that time that the judge yielded to their appeals and agreed to the yearly exhibition. Naturally, he found a way to profit from his concession. I suppose I do not need to tell you that all his actions were at all times premeditated to serve his purposes.

'With the proper strategy, even the most difficult opponent can be defeated,' they would often hear him mumbling as he wandered on his own in the huge corridors of the palace.

Well, every year at this time, the Castle of Perfection welcomed familiar faces and conducted art contests. Each and every person had the right to participate, given the fact that what distinguished our judge, more than anything else, was his 'highly democratic mentality.'

He actually lived for that comparison. For that holy moment when the unveiling ceremonies would underscore the superiority of his magnificent society. The mediocre ones would lower their heads, and the once timid boy would mete out thunders. A puff of perfection filled the mediocre masses with envy, and this envy, like a cactus, put up with its own thorns.

He had not seen his adopted daughter in days. After their argument, she had completely devoted herself to her artistic work.

'You will admire my work, along with the rest. You truly deserve a nice surprise,' she had informed him in their last meeting.

What a girl, Compulsion thought with a smile on his face.

She was actually not such a bad kid. Once in a while, she was badly influenced by her association with the cobbler, but she would soon become wiser and carry out her duties without mumbling and grumbling.

He had come to the conclusion that young people do need a good scolding once in a while. Of course, there was no doubt that his daughter would bring glory to him once again through her prolific talent and her amazing creations.

The most perfect of the perfect ones suddenly felt his tie suffocating him. Damned symptoms! He had suffered from them since childhood. Yet, he never deigned to seek help from the top psychoanalyst. Panic attacks. A new trend. The perfect ones often met to find a solution to this problem. You see, they still failed to perceive that they were destined for triumph and not for happiness.

The judge tightened his tie even more. Just out of spite. Then he opened the door of his house. History was awaiting their appointment. It would not be long now. He was renowned for his punctuality.

ELEVEN

The golden gates opened just as the scarlet sun was taking its leave from the sky.

From the highest balcony of the palace, the photographer hastened to capture on camera the historic encounter of day and night.

'Light and darkness walk hand in hand eternally. They fight with each other; they befriend each other. They are born; they die. They pull the strings of our destinies. They may bring our destinies down, and they may raise them high. They may crush us, but they may also glorify us,' he told himself as the wind was disheveling his hair.

The mediocre ones and the perfect ones. The distance that existed between them was, for now, eradicated. For one night. For that particular night. For as long as the dream drapes with a magic veil, the nostalgia for the past. Embraces that are both warm and desperate, just like the steps of the dancers who are well aware that they have only one more tune to dance to.

'Let us laugh aloud
over all that brought us together in the past.
One night seems too little,

but it does make life seem worthwhile.' The cobbler was singing in the corner, accompanying himself with a guitar.

A tall, slim, blonde young woman, dressed in white from head to toe, reluctantly approached the famous heart surgeon and softly touched him on the shoulder. He turned toward her and took her in his arms, longingly.

'You are turning into an attractive woman. You hardly ever come to visit me, the stranger in the Castle. The kind words in your letters do soothe my sorrow a bit. Nevertheless, I do not forgive myself. For your first smudges in the school notebooks, for the schoolbag that was far too heavy for your delicate shoulders, for the anxieties that you never shared with me, for the good times that I was never there to witness, for the gloomy afternoons that I could not convert into celebrations with colorful balloons, for all the things that have passed us by and can never be brought back. For all these things, I do not forgive myself,' he said, out of breath.

The young woman put his hand in hers in a protective manner.

'Missions set up barricades. The more sublime the missions, the more final the goodbyes, I believe. I may not have grown up by your side, but I do take pride in your accomplishments from afar. In a strange way, I always feel you nearby. I close my eyes, and I touch you in my sweetest dreams, those where the golden gates remain wide open, and the bold hearts defy segregations. So don't cry,' she said, trying to raise his spirits.

Meanwhile, there was music all around; the notes seemed to sprinkle the relationships with bitter sugar. Friends, parents, children, and lovers got all tangled up. Dancing loves equality. This is one thing they would learn with the passing of time.

The melodies suddenly stopped as if someone muzzled them up violently.

'Ladies and gentlemen, you are cordially invited to the art gallery. Artists from all over the world will now exhibit their works. The judges have already taken their seats at the front table. Let us enjoy the evening,' the king announced over the microphone, giving the people time to recover from their highly emotional state as he did every year. The performance was about to commence.

TWELVE

Behind the stage, the artists were impatiently awaiting their turn. The names were called out over the microphone, and the paintings were placed onto the stage with extreme care. The artists then gave a brief introduction and proceeded with the unveiling of their works.

Judge Compulsion's adopted daughter felt she was short of breath. Her hands were trembling, and her heart was beating loudly. Shortly before the fatal leap, she felt fear returning threateningly and flirting with steep cliffs. Once again, light was struggling against darkness, and the young woman was about to choose her orbit either around the sun or among the clouds.

A loud voice interrupted her thoughts.

'You are a lucky one! You have no worries at all! Everyone is at your feet, and your reputation has reached places you had never imagined in your wildest childhood dreams.'

The artist turned to face the piercing voice. A girl, dressed in black clothes, with sad, dark eyes and disheveled hair, was looking at her with some envy and a great deal of bitterness.

'We forget that the soulless dolls of the shop windows pine for an escape from their glittering clothes,' she replied gently.

The artist in black turned her back scornfully and added the last touches to her mediocre drawing.

On the stage, an amiable young man, wearing a wrinkled red shirt and blue corduroy pants, was fraught with anxiety over the opinion of the impartial judges regarding his work.

'My dear, your butterflies are sweet, but the log cabin evokes pity,' Judge Compulsion commented gloatingly.

The young man moved his left leg nervously for a while. Then he mumbled a humble 'thank you' and ran off, whisking his immature talent off to the world of the invisible, exactly where it had always belonged.

At some point, the name of the judge's adopted daughter was announced. She knew very well that she was about to leave behind the fog and move toward clear skies. She advanced forward in a determined way and stood proudly in the center of the stage.

'I will not waste your time, although, with the right company, I have a propensity for chattering away. Our king says that our actions speak louder than words. I wholeheartedly agree. You know, artists flirt shamelessly with the elusive and the magical. The boldest ones get rid of the deceptive wrappings and reveal the empty contents. I, myself, will always be creating for all those people who untie the fancy ribbons and remove the wrapping paper in order to get to the content.'

The curtain was then suddenly pulled back, and the sleepwalker got rid of the safety pillows. What was revealed to the onlookers was a gray, dilapidated castle with skeletons jumping out of the luxurious closets. The gold garments had turned into cells that imprisoned the figures of the perfect ones in their deceptive glow, while the sorrowful faces sharply underlined the discord that existed in the ideal society.

Judge Compulsion opened his eyes wide and kept chewing his tie nervously. Silence fell in the crowd. A horrible storm was taking place outside, and you could swear that the rainwater was seeping through the solid walls of the building, arousing the living dead.

What was in store for them on the next day, and which castle would set the truth free?

A tune prolonged the mystery in the atmosphere.

'Tick-tock, the clock strikes;

the hourglass is flowing,

and the pieces are set in order.

Tick-tock, a journey commences

for all those who clearly perceived the painting.'

THIRTEEN

The storm had finally subsided, while a cluster of clouds seemed to be awaiting the inevitable signal. The sun and the stars were walking side by side again, anticipating a setting and a rising, an end and a new start. At the Castle of Perfection, the ideal professionals shut themselves up in their rooms, anxious over the judge's verdict.

The photographer kept going over that fateful moment again and again. The magnificent painting was unveiled, and the bewildered crowd was blinded by its rays of light. The truth was that the judge had not 'read' the young woman accurately. She really had guts. She defied the king's rules and turned her brush into a magic wand. Deep down, he was somewhat envious of her. He himself had been putting his head down and obeying orders, seducing the joy of creation with rules rather than inspiration.

Who knows what kind of punishment Judge Compulsion had in store for his adopted daughter? The photographer was observing him closely during the whole incident. Underneath the starched shirt and the expensive jacket, he saw a pitiful figure that was shaking all over and walking unsteadily.

'The presentation is over. Return to your homes,' he had said, almost stuttering.

The photographer felt sorry for him. By then, everyone had seen the painting. No matter what his verdict would be, history was plunging into uncharted waters, and there was no safe turning back. They would either drown in the rough sea or tame the current.

At the other end of the building, our artist was awake and counting the hours until she would have to face the king's wrath. Three knocks on the door interrupted her thoughts.

Cheron, she supposed and rushed to open the door. He stood facing her and just watched her as she was folding her sweating palms nervously and smiling at him awkwardly. Then, he applauded her for quite a while.

'I take my hat off to you, in truth,

for your courage that is huge.

Do not fret over the consequences.

You attain happiness with your own arrow,' he said.

A young girl had once come through the gate. She did not have much confidence in herself and her strength at the time, but Cheron had seen it in her eyes. She was definitely the one. She was the one who would take hold of the stars with both hands. The cobbler patiently let the seasons pass by, nature die and come to life again, the perfect ones sacrifice heartbeats and punish flaws. Spring would eventually come. Spring always came for the restless and the authentic, for the damned and the romantic, for all those who do not make do with tight shoes and do not waste their brushes on spiritless, lifeless paintings.

On the previous night, a fairy godmother saved the fairy tale. Dressed in the colors of the rainbow, she shook her blonde hair gracefully and shouted out an old secret.

'Do not count on his mercy

and do not settle for favors.

You, yourself, determine your destiny,

and the steering wheel will lead you anywhere you wish,' he whispered to her with tearful eyes.

'If only I could leave the Castle behind for good and go wherever my heart takes me,' the artist mumbled.

'That is actually up to you.

If you wish it very much,

it will happen at once,' he encouraged her.

'They will stop me. There is no doubt that the iron gate will obstruct the course of my dreams.'

'All of us are, in fact, born free.

We are put in chains by nonexistent fears,' her eccentric friend now reminded her.

The melody finally burst the balloon of lies. The artist remembered that old group of friends, quite a long time back, sitting in a circle and having a discussion.

'What is fear?' one would wonder out loud.

'Nothing more than the cage of our mind,' another one answered with certainty.

'Shall we give in to it?' a third one broke in.

'We will hold on to the keys even when we are deceived into believing that we lost them for good,' added the fourth one.

The young woman opened the bedside table drawer with determination and touched her piece of the miniature castle. Who knows? Maybe she would meet them again. Now she knew well what she had to do. She declared herself free. She always was—we always are.

She gave Cheron a warm embrace.

'Thank you for your wise tunes, for loosening shoes with self-sacrifice, and for healing broken wings. I will not forget you. I am just going to turn the page. I hope to see you again. Somewhere else. At a more beautiful and less perfect place.'

'Defy the monster,

and let go of the canes.

The spiders and the skeletons

have only deceptive power.' The cobbler was singing as the young woman got farther and farther away.

She walked boldly and reached the huge gate. The robust guards firmly blocked her way.

'Open up!' she shouted.

They immediately stepped aside, and a bright sun welcomed the artist. Judge Compulsion was watching her from his balcony but could not stop her. Fear had tied her hands, and insight was untying them.

FOURTEEN

Do not ask what is outside this prison. My dear child, the world is sinking in its contradictions, it is taking account of its mistakes, and it is consumed by its huge passions. Yet you should make a point of moving forward at all times. Forgive the past, and it will loosen its noose around your neck. And, in the silence, you might one day realize deep down that we are all gods and demons at the same time. Paradise and hell are wrestling inside us from the dawn to the sunset of our mortal existence. Nevertheless, there is hope. I feel it more strongly now than ever. If you are redeemed, then maybe you can redeem us. You will do it for yourself, of course, but one day—do make a note of this—there will be a lot of us. An army of free people who defied the rules. One day. Years now, the same thought keeps me alive and going. The someday that will become now. A long journey is awaiting you. Uphill, downhill, agonizing puffing and huffing and intoxicating euphoria. Do not extol the straight roads. You walk more indolently on paved roads. Do not get angry when you encounter obstacles. It is the obstacles that have brought you to this point today. So I will see you again where the breaths we take prove us worthy of our lives—that is when we shall meet again.'

Many miles away from the Castle, the artist kept bringing to mind the words of the director. She had sneaked into his prison cell just a few minutes before her final getaway. She had been longing to see him for quite some time. His hair had turned completely white. He was thin and emaciated, but his eyes remained serene. A wise man who managed to conquer the oxygen with enslaved lungs, he was the one she had always truly admired.

'Fear the invisible prison cells,' were the final words he whispered to her.

Nature was now laying generous gifts at her feet, and she was impatient to do away with the redundant ribbons.

'Everything in its time,

catch the train on time at its station,' the cobbler would often sing to her, extolling the virtue of patience.

The initial feeling of euphoria was quickly succeeded by an agitation she had never felt before. The trembling of her whole body and the knot in the throat were again having a heyday. She was in the middle of nowhere without an inkling as to what she should do next. She stood motionless for a while and weighed her options. The wind ruffled her golden curls and absolved the sins of all the feathers that succumbed to its charm. The landscape strove to soothe her anxiety with colorful flowers.

'Close your eyes and listen to me,

then with a pure heart follow me.' It seemed to be whispering.

The young woman started to wander aimlessly. She was not looking, yet she was able to see more clearly. She just followed beauty and this, in a strange way, seemed sufficient. At one point, she decided to rest near a spring with burbling water. She wanted to quench her thirst and gather courage for the remaining journey. At the other side of the spring, a squirrel was doing its best to lay claim to her attention. It was jumping from one branch to the other until it finally landed on her shoulder.

'Trust me.' She could swear it whispered to her, but then again, it could have been the rustling of the leaves that had started a conversation with her imagination.

The charming animal was now leading her uphill. The orange sun was setting at the top.

The end and the beginning, she thought.

A round sign warned in big, red letters: 'The Lands of Emotions.'

A huge fence protected against the indiscreet. In the center, there was a door. Green. Just like our most sacred hopes. On its surface, a number of words challenged all the visitors who were on a quest for answers:

'What is gnawing at you day and night,

but if the upside is turned down

the universe it will rebuild afresh?'

She remembered she had always had a problem with riddles and concluded that this one would be no exception to the rule. The squirrel lay down by her side as if it were anticipating something—a decision and a new route. The artist took a deep breath and opened the door widely. Adventure would now match its forces against her riddle.

FIFTEEN

She looked around, carefully observing the place in which she found herself. People were flooding the streets, deep in thought. Where could they be going, and what could they be looking for? The skyscrapers seemed to be in a constant vendetta with infinity, and the clouds gave an outlet to their rage through rainstorms.

The artist wandered for a while in the gloomy landscape that tortured the souls like an inhospitable god. Eventually, she stopped at a centrally located pastry shop and asked for some ice-cream with her favorite flavors, strawberry and bitter chocolate—joys and sorrows.

Upon leaving, she patiently waited at the traffic light. Just as she was about to cross the street, a hand held her back. Frightened, she turned and came face to face with a pretty woman with black wavy hair and blue eyes. She was wearing a long yellow dress.

'Who are you?' Compulsion's adopted daughter asked her.

The stranger patted her gently on the shoulder, and this magic touch allayed the artist's suspiciousness and mistrust.

'The people who live in the lands of emotions stand out for their hospitality. Do you think we would leave you alone in a place to which you are a stranger? Our visitors deserve a warm welcome and some encouraging words. Anyway, without visitors, our new society cannot get ahead. We pamper our visitors, we love them and, above all, we respect their maps.'

'So where are we off to?' the artist said, her mood having been uplifted.

'You are smiling. That means you trust me.'

'I do believe that I will need a friend here. Besides, I have no sense of direction in unfamiliar places.'

'I see that you are exorcising your demons with humor. You have had this skill from a very young age.'

'You sound as if you know me,' the artist wondered.

'The fact is that all of us both know and don't know each other. We are at the same time acquaintances and strangers, friends and enemies, parents and children. We constantly try on different roles in our attempt to trick time.'

'I guess it is my destiny to hang out with odd people,' the artist grumbled in response.

'You hold all the answers. Don't try to attribute what happens to you to divine intervention. Also, avoid advice.'

Yet the latter did sound like advice.

'It seems that the humans have passed on their bad habits to me.'

'The humans? If I cannot include you in this category, does it mean I have the honor of talking to a fairy godmother? Strange things are happening today, and I get the impression that I am in the realm of a dream world,' the artist retorted.

'What if you are actually just waking up from a dream?' the stranger challenged her.

'I will accept it as just another possibility. In fact, there are infinite possibilities, practically as many as our paths. That is what an old friend once told me.'

'Why don't we take a walk? But, of course, only if you agree. I do not make a habit of imposing my presence on people.'

'Of course, I agree. Now tell me, does your dense cloud cover sightseeing, or is there nothing more here than gray buildings?'

The pretty tour guide laughed heartily. 'The cloud helps you appreciate the days when there is visibility. You can count it as an ally, then. Actually, our walk will involve discussing the nature and fate of people rather than sightseeing.'

'I always observe them carefully.'

'Great! Shall we begin?'

The two women started their walk in the gray landscape.

'Your name is Quirky.'

'Did you see this in your magic ball?'

'We all have a magic ball. It is just that we have not been taught how to read it,' the pretty woman answered mysteriously.

'And who are you?' the artist wanted to know.

'They call me Sixth Sense.'

'An unusual name.'

'At one time, it used to be popular, but it has gradually been discarded.'

'I suppose trends come and go just like the fretful crowds in this place.'

'You immediately recognized the load you are carrying on your own back. Anxiety and agony are your burden. The crowds just remind you of so many sleepless nights of yours.'

'The noose that tightens around my neck,' Quirky admitted.

'Why don't you loosen it a bit?'

'I ran away from the Castle with the hope of doing just that. What if every corner of the universe, however, has imprisoned the colors, thereby robbing me of my life?'

'The river has two banks,' the mysterious woman answered.

'I have been stuck on the same riverbank for years,' the artist bitterly concluded.

'You insist on carrying your past along.'

'Why don't I get rid of useless baggage?'

'You fear freedom more than anything else.'

Quirky strongly disagreed. 'But I seek freedom.'

'Naturally. The journey would not have started had it not been for this basic desire of yours. You crave freedom, and simultaneously, you fear it in the same way that we always fear the unknown, the sublime and lofty, the top, the view from the top,' Sixth Sense concluded.

'I touch freedom, but then it always gets away from me,' Quirky said sorrowfully.

'The hourglass is working in your favor, and you will soon rest by the spring. But let us return to our subject. You mentioned that you love to observe people.'

'Yes, they fascinate and inspire me.'

'Do you remember faces?' The stranger caught her off guard.

'I won't forget yours if that is what you are asking me.'

'Actually, I have a mission for you. Your mission will be to comprehend and analyze the inner world of some passersby.'

'It sounds quite interesting.'

'Great. Look around you then. We have already reached the train station. You would not call this the ideal place to take you on a sightseeing tour, but remember that I have assigned a project to you. Three passengers. That is how many I want.'

'Ready,' the artist informed her after a few minutes.

'I am listening.'

'Behind you, on the left, there is a teenager with reddish-brown hair. He is standing and constantly looking at his watch. The moment is slipping by him, but he is just shrouding the seasons with ingratitude.'

'What does he remind you of?' Sixth Sense insisted.

'Every sunrise in my life and the one yesterday that did not have time to go to its setting,' Quirky surmised bitterly.

'An insightful observation. Let us move on.'

'In front of you is a hunched-over woman with completely white hair who is struggling to solve a crossword puzzle. The horizontal and vertical clues are mourning along with her for all the things she lost before she even got the chance to live through them. Ah, to feel the approaching of spring when you will scatter your half-finished affairs to eternity! A distressing awareness, no doubt. Death is a skeleton that haunts one's nights. The human being, the only creature that is aware of being given this bitter ultimatum…' The artist sighed deeply.

'You just cannot stand it,' Sixth Sense said in a low voice.

'Who can stand it?' Quirky replied, startled by the question.

'A painful and precious lesson.'

'Precious?'

'You know, I often wonder about you, my dear. Since you were not created immortal, why don't you celebrate your every waking moment? Sleep comes and seals your eyelids more sweetly after celebrations.'

'I tend to believe that we are born unfulfilled and insatiable.'

'Every river is flanked by two banks,' the mysterious woman reminded her.

'Your favorite phrase.'

'You will soon make it yours too.'

'Three. That is how many passengers you have asked me to describe.' The judge's adopted daughter went back to the subject at hand.

'Continue,' Sixth Sense urged her.

'The young woman at the last bench. She cannot be over twenty. She has set off for school, yet she is not really aware of where she is actually going. She is holding a pen in her hand, and she is writing something in her little notebook. Then she rips the page out in despair and throws it into the trash bin. She is locking horns with her thoughts as if she is trying to give shape to shadows and confront the invisible.'

'She has yet to achieve this.'

'Yes. She has not been able to do so yet,' Quirky agreed.

'We are leaving,' the stranger informed her.

'Where are we going now?'

'It is time to cross the river.'

'Here we go again!'

'You will understand,' Sixth Sense assured her.

They put behind them highways and shops, hurried passersby and nervous drivers, until the river stretched out before them like a sumptuous tray. A boatman was waiting for them patiently, as if his breath were justified only by the sacred act of taking travelers to their destination. Silent during the whole voyage, he signaled the end of it with a gesture. The gesture seemed to be a thank you for being allowed to be instrumental in straightening out destinies.

On the opposite bank, nature, embroidered with colorful flowers, seemed to be deeply bowing to the two women. The birds were chirping cheerfully, and the little houses, situated close to each other, filled the heart with an unprecedented sense of intimacy.

'It is beautiful here,' the artist remarked.

'There is this world as well. It is actually not so far off from the old one. From the infamous noose that is threatening your neck.'

A teenager in a flowery shirt and worn-out jeans was rolling lightheartedly in the grass. Quirky had no trouble recognizing him. The young man was playing the guitar and breaking one clock after another.

'A melody I am happily whispering,

and more time to the hands of the clock I am refusing,' he sang.

A bit further down, the grandmother from the train station was making bread on a counter while two children were embroidering their moves with all kinds of teasing and games. Death was curling up in his cave, but even if he, like a pirate, decided on a sudden attack, he would not be able to inflict harm on the lovers of the present time.

The bewildered girl from the bench was now resting under an old plane tree, holding a book in her hands.

'May it fare well!' friends and acquaintances wished her.

She seemed proud and composed. She had confided her nightmares in the paper, and she had come to terms with the shadows. They would not harm her, and she would not wage war on them—a decent agreement.

'Well?' Sixth Sense brought the artist out of her silence.

'The passengers locked the bad witch in the coach of the train,' Quirky noted.

'What if the good fairy and the bad witch are one and the same?' the woman retorted.

'Ah, Good and Evil. The eternal battle.'

'We really should not get involved in fights.'

'How else can we be crowned with success?' the judge's adopted daughter wondered.

'We succeed every minute that we honor life rather than the invisible tyrants,' the tour guide replied.

'I would do anything to draw out their secrets,' Quirky said, manifesting her desire.

'It would prove to be a losing battle. We put up with uphill climbing before we rest at the top.'

'I chose to describe two artists. I wonder if that is a coincidence.'

'There are no coincidences. The artist, an odd architect we might as well call him, constructs new worlds. He creates magical skies and crosses them with his wings. I must correct you on something, though. You chose three artists, not two. Even the grandmother who makes bread belongs to this category. Do not forget that the rhapsodists of dreams bless our paths with bright colors, splendid fragrances, delicious flavors, and warm embraces.'

'Change is just a matter of making a decision,' the artist concluded.

'Just a boat ride away,' Sixth Sense pointed out.

'Since I boarded the boat, there is no danger of my going back, is there?'

'Difficult question. We are constantly born, and we constantly die. On foggy days, we flirt with setbacks, but we don't easily lose sight of the clear skies that once dissolved the bleak darkness. So we find them again.'

'And the noose around the neck?' Quirky asked apprehensively.

'Are you thinking about it?'

'It is suffocating me.'

'You will loosen it as soon as you perceive that it does not serve a purpose. When its purpose has been fulfilled, it becomes a harmless ghost.'

The night spread its charm on the world, and the carefree interludes seduced countless wishes.

'The time has passed. You still have a long way to go,' the tour guide reminded Quirky.

'Aren't you coming along?' Quirky pleaded with her.

'I cannot follow in your footsteps.'

'I will always remember you. You have given me so much in such little time.' The artist expressed her gratitude.

'I have given you nothing more than what you were carrying in your soul.'

'So a boat will be sailing in the river even in the heaviest of winters,' the young woman recapitulated.

'You will discern it when your heart desires it.'

'And then the other bank of the river will shower my hopes with stars.'

'The stars will always be falling in our hands when we invite them.'

'Goodbye.'

'Goodbyes are unnecessary. I have become part of you, and I will accompany you from now on.'

***

At that very moment, somewhere far away, a colorful dot danced in the air a little and then landed in the blank painting, adorning it with one word: 'Creation.'

'How in the world did this happen?' Compulsion mumbled at the top floor of the Castle. Sweat was trickling down his forehead as he was struggling for quite a while to erase the letters in the untouched-by-human-hand canvas. Needless to say, his attempts were futile.

SIXTEEN

Quirky walked for hours in the vast desert. Although the long walk had tired her, she obstinately persisted in pulling her heavy legs forward. She was very thirsty. Sweat was running down her face, and its beads colored her anticipation with a myriad of hopes.

During all this time, she would often bring to mind her brief walk with the stranger, a symbol of the passersby who smile and befriend us. What a long story. What a strange story. All these people are not part of our everyday life, but they transform it with their pithy words and their weighty actions.

Soon her attention was drawn by a sign: 'Four kilometers.'

The next country was now just a breath away. She was hoping that someone would welcome her soon and exchange some words with her. She had always loved company. Not the company that provides your bruised palate with cheap alcohol and shallow compliments but the company that smashes glass cups and flows just like an unimpeded river.

Actually, there was no time for daydreaming. A lofty mission was calling her on to yet another important path, and the green door emerged again in the middle of nowhere, awaiting a new meeting.

'What penetrates the skin and rejuvenates the heart?' was the question at hand.

She felt as if she were fumbling in the dark for the prison keys; nevertheless, with her head high, she bid the desert farewell. She walked quite a while longer until she discerned a small tavern in the distance. It looked anything but hostile. The tables were set out by the sea as if they were daring the next big wave to pull them into the heart of the sea. The customers, in groups, were absorbed in their discussions, drinking and scoffing at death from their high-spirited hideouts.

The sun and the clouds seemed to be having a showdown, and it was far too risky to bet on which would prevail. The traveler made herself comfortable at the end table and took out a book. The title was *The Tight Shoes*, and it was her loot from her previous destination. The girl she saw on the train had written it, and a friend of hers had forgotten it by the old plane tree.

'We really should return it to him,' she had said upon finding it.

'Keep it. Obviously, it has fallen into your hands for a purpose,' Sixth Sense had advised her.

Tight shoes. She had had experience with them in many ways. There had been, as a matter of fact, many such shoes in her old closet. Mostly such shoes, if we are to be precise. Who could actually know this? It could be that everyone walks in tight shoes. We get so used to them that we eventually forget our right size.

'Wake up. Are you going to order something, or am I just wasting my time here?' a hoarse voice said.

Quirky jumped up and saw a young man her age standing in front of her. His brown hair was shoulder length, and his dark eyes were showering the place with a charming audacity. He smiled at her.

'Wow! You frighten easily. You were on the verge of plunging into the sea.'

'Sorry. My mind was wandering elsewhere,' she apologized.

'I have never seen you around here before.'

'I am just passing through.'

'Oh, I too once started out on an adventure, but the journey tired me, and I settled down here.' He opened up to her.

'Have you built a home here?'

'If there can be homes without brick roofs.'

'And how are you faring?'

'Great! I have devoted myself to this tavern of mine. Customers come in groups, they try my fine wine, and they spice up their lives with my dishes. People don't need a lot of things to make them happy. Things are simple; we complicate them.'

'Could it be that we enjoy torturing ourselves?' the judge's adopted daughter wondered.

'We take ourselves seriously. We consider ourselves important or, at least, we strive to do so. We crave social recognition, wealth, and glory. Not for our sake, don't fool yourself. Basically, we do it so we can show off to our social circle. Just a dot in infinity that will complete its orbit; that's what we all are.'

'What about love? Doesn't it give us flavors of immortality?'

'Of course it does if it is allowed to roam around freely. However, we defile it every single minute, and we name the cuffs wedding bands.

'Cynical.'

'Just realistic.'

'Do you feel the same absolute contempt for relationships as you do for married life?'

'Man was not born for monogamy, my friend. This is the only truth that I can pass on to everyone with certainty. I was struggling with this matter for a long time, but here I have found myself.'

Quirky was confounded. 'Have I come to the land of the confirmed bachelors?'

'You can put it that way if you must have labels. In these areas, we tend to do whatever our heart desires. Today I sleep with you to satisfy my passion, but tomorrow I may wake up feeling differently. In that case, I owe you nothing. I pick up my hat and sign my departure. Simple. Everything is simple. I am repeating this to you in the hope that you can grasp it.'

'Do you people have children, or do you avoid such responsibilities?'

'Even the worst form of vanity does not, in any way, point to the perpetuation of the species.'

'Nonetheless, this mentality will only lead to your world disappearing from the map. You will grow old, and obviously, you will… ' She hesitated for a while.

'Come on, why don't you say it outright? Are you afraid that Death is eavesdropping and will grab you sooner?' The young tavern owner laughed heartily.

'Will I ever eat?' The artist winked at him, changing the subject.

'You are definitely in the right place for that. Hell, I got carried away with our discussion. You are such a babbler,' he teased her.

'I didn't take the words out of you by force.'

'You drew me into the discussion, I must admit. Time to work! I'll be back with lots of tasty dishes.'

'Aren't you going to take my order first?' the young woman wondered.

'Enough is enough. In my tavern, I serve people whatever my heart desires,' he informed her with a smile.

'Very democratic of you!'

'The secret of my charm. One of the many. How about going for a walk as soon as I close my tavern today? I have the feeling that you will get lost on your own, my charming daydreamer.'

'Why don't I have something to eat first, and we will talk about that later.' It was her turn to tease him.

Soon the last customers said their goodbyes to the tavern owner. They left in a lighter spirit, walking somewhat unsteadily from the drinking and the good time. Quirky had more than enjoyed her delicious food and now expressed her eagerness to explore the new and unfamiliar country.

The young man sat across from her.

'Will you ever get up from that chair?' he asked her as he moved her chair back and forth playfully.

'You don't treat your guests that well, do you?' the artist remarked.

'Pretentious good manners bore me to tears. How about you?' He provoked her.

'I fully agree with you.'

'Come on, then. Get up!' he urged her.

'Where are we going?'

'We will meet our own history, or rather, to be more accurate, we will create it ourselves. This country is small, and I aspire to walk you through it all,' he answered in a very serious tone.

'What is worth seeing more than anything else here?'

'I have always believed that the most significant journeys are those that bring us closer to ourselves,' the young man answered earnestly.

'The most significant as well as the most time-consuming,' she agreed. 'However, I only have a few hours at my disposal, and quite a lot of kilometers are waiting for me to cross them. As soon as the tour is over, therefore, you will hear my goodbye,' she informed him.

'We will walk very slowly then so that I can get enough of you unless I come to wish to get rid of you soon because of your babbling. In that case, we will rush through it. Can you at least run fast?'

'In the school races, I was always in last place.'

'I am not surprised in the least.'

'And why is that, may I ask?'

'Speed makes you dizzy,' he conjectured.

'It is true. We forgot to introduce ourselves to each other, however,' Quirky pointed out.

'There is no reason for that. We are more effectively introduced through our words.'

'And what do they call you?'

'I turn to all the names.'

'I will call you Mister Nobody then.'

'No objections to that. Let's set off! Take your jacket. The weather may seem pleasant now, but at night the wind wakes up from its lethargy and pierces the skin.'

***

They walked together, two strangers that had so much to say to each other. The names were put aside. 'People get to know each other better without their prisons,' the cobbler used to say.

A vast sea flirted with eternity, and they were dancing barefoot next to it, while the waters barely managed to touch their feet.

'We haven't seen any houses yet, only tents here and there!'

'We live in tents.'

'Don't you long for a brick roof over your head?'

'Bricks, just like commitments, press down on us,' Nobody declared.

'You run away from them.'

'Exactly. Whenever we feel like it, we take our tent and go. Without resorting to any kind of drama.'

'How did you and so many other odd ones end up together?'

'How did you reach the decision to travel?' he retorted.

'I reckon I was forced into it because of a need.'

'This is true for all of us. To sleep more serenely at night, this is what we all pray for. But tell me, have you ever fallen in love?' he asked indiscreetly.

'No. But I do dream of love.'

'You are a romantic one then.'

'"The romantics rebuild the Earth from scratch," a friend of mine used to sing.'

'We choose our lyrics, and, as a result, we carry the responsibility for them on our shoulders,' he remarked.

'Do you have a river here?' she wanted to know.

'What kind of question is that? The wild sea is inviting you to explore it, and you are craving for freshwater,' he said almost reproachfully.

'Answer my question,' Quirky insisted.

'We do. Actually, that is where our community ends. Every afternoon I see from the same distance the same boatman. He seems to be wasting his time, to have given in to laziness. For all I know, he may be waiting for something. Once in a great while, he does take travelers to the other side of the river.'

'Has anyone from your community ever crossed the river?' the artist inquired.

'Some woman did.'

'Was it the woman you loved?'

'Curiosity killed the cat.'

'I doubt it. Curiosity saved the cat,' she corrected him. 'Why didn't you follow her?' she asked him after a few minutes of silence.

'We were having a fine time together. I don't know what got into her head and made her want us to leave. I, for one, consider this land my home, and I don't easily abandon my home.' He made it clear to her.

'Did you get scared?'

'It may have happened just that way. Are you satisfied now that you have solved the riddle?'

'You are frightened of love. It will eventually bid you goodbye, and you will stay behind counting your tears. You will be in pain. You are avoiding pain.'

'It has not led me astray. I don't get very close, and I whistle indifferently when it comes to drama.'

'You trick your despondency by running away from tender embraces.'

'Embraces stifle me.'

'Obviously. You put your identity at risk in warm embraces.'

'So, which identity do I hold on to?'

'The identity of the easygoing man whom nothing touches or transforms.'

'You are squeezing your mind in vain. It is best that you come to terms with whatever does not lend itself to change.'

'We are approaching the river,' the artist thought out loud as the water was now in sight.

'What an obsession! We will be there in a few minutes,' he assured her.

'Let's cross it together. Please don't refuse me this favor,' she pleaded with him.

'I still have some time at my disposal to decide on that. For now, I suggest that we just enjoy our walk. That is what we agreed on to begin with,' he answered.

'It has become quite chilly,' she complained, changing the subject of conversation.

For quite some time, she was struggling to take her jacket out of her backpack, but it had got firmly stuck to the zipper. She pulled at it five times with all her strength and hardly any patience. She finally removed it and covered her shoulders with relief.

'You dropped something,' her friend pointed out immediately and picked up an object wrapped in aluminum foil from the ground.

'Give it to me!' she shouted, while her face turned red in agitation.

'Have you got your dowry here or just some food scraps for the road?' he teased her.

'This is the only object that I must never lose,' she mumbled.

'It must be something very important. Can I see it?' He lowered his voice.

'I consider it very personal,' she snapped at him.

'I trusted you a few minutes ago and confided my life story to you,' he reminded her while curiosity was clumsily scratching his adrenalin.

'Unwrap it, if you insist,' she conceded resignedly.

He was soon holding the piece of the castle in his hand. His face was smudged with puzzlement. For a while, he just stared at her. He found it impossible to utter a word. He slowly pulled the string that was hiding underneath his shirt. The second part of the castle was brought to the surface of the new era.

Quirky, frozen, found it impossible to move in any direction. She stood still in the same spot, in that yard that had been deprived of springs and in that long winter that seemed to be finally retreating.

'Cynic!' she mumbled after a while.

'Quirky!' he responded.

Then the two of them were in each other's arms and refused to part for quite some time. Their hide-and-seek had finally come to a happy end, and the trees gave crops longing for the fragrant flowers of innocence.

'Time was passing, and the hope to meet you all was fading away,' Cynic revealed and clasped his friend's hand affectionately.

'It never died down. You have been carrying us around in a locket for years. You are not as cynical as you would have people believe after all.'

'Possibly. I am beginning to believe in miracles. You desired to cross a river. Shall we cross it together?' he suddenly suggested.

Just a hundred meters away, the silent boatman was actually waiting for them. He gladly took them to the other side of the river. He even treated them to a warm, almost sympathetic wink when they reached their destination.

On the other bank of the river, the bright sun was gradually giving way to the emerging moon. On their way, they came across familiar little shops. No houses, only tents all around.

'I was wrong to fear the boat ride. I feel as if I am walking in my homeland.' The young man felt relief.

They soon met the first residents there. Carefree hippies gathered around a big fire were carving their sorrows in the sand and then diving into the sea. Folklore has it that every time a swimmer stepped his wet feet on the land, part of his grief disappeared, and a great joy was about to come his way.

A bit further off, an elderly couple were gazing at the moon in each other's arms. Quirky approached them.

'I apologize for my boldness, but I would really love to talk to you.'

'My beautiful young lady, your apologies are not necessary. Interaction with young people actually rejuvenates old people like us. After all, we have vowed to blow out our birthday candles without shortness of breath,' the old man retorted.

'You seem to be very happy together.'

'We have recently celebrated our sixtieth anniversary. The one eases the other's path on nights when we mourn for our mortal nature. We all experience such nights, don't you fool yourself about this. Love helps us deal with it a little better,' the woman continued.

'Fate has sprinkled you with heaps of good luck. Love usually considers time an enemy,' Cynic remarked.

'We do not pass by souls hurriedly here. We soften their dark phases and extol their light ones,' the old man answered.

'What a great risk. It is a futile investment since it is going to end up in the ground,' the young man pointed out, looking almost suspiciously at the elderly couple.

'Actually, it is the only worthwhile risk. Nonetheless, I must admit that you have a point. Human beings do depart. Yet, they do not die. They dance in the pages of our books, in the lyrics that we hummed together and in confessions that justified the drawers of history,' the old woman answered, and Cynic's face immediately softened up.

Quirky watched her old friend closely.

Whoever manages to perceive even once finds it impossible to forget. She remembered the cobbler's words.

The two childhood friends bid the elderly couple a warm goodbye and continued on their way. The sky had by then gotten quite dark.

'I must continue my journey,' the young woman hesitantly announced.

'Keep the goodbyes for later. I am coming with you.' Cynic startled her.

'There will be many steep climbs, and they can rob you of your breath.'

'We need to find the other two parts,' he reminded her.

'Do you think we will find them?'

'We will at least try. Yes. Just for old times' sake.'

Having said this, the two of them set off toward the path that was steep and painful, high and lofty, a path that does not forgive cowardice but redeems bravery.

***

Meanwhile, Judge Compulsion, alone at the dinner table, was going through the motions of chewing his food but without much of an appetite as the once blank painting, placed directly across his seat, was eating away at his ego. All of a sudden, the brush came to life again. It grabbed the judge's bite and fork and turned them into red paint that added another word to the canvas: 'Love.'

At the same time, a very loud noise penetrated every corner of the Castle, and an earthquake shook the architectural wonder to its foundations. The chandeliers were dancing wildly, and various objects were thrown around in the rooms, the corridors, and the stairways. The perfect ones were curling up apprehensively under the sturdy tables. They were praying for the nightmare to end so that they could return to their excellent, orderly life and their numerous awards. They were praying that they would not have occasion to pray again as having to invoke someone who was more powerful than themselves made them feel quite weak and uncomfortable.

The cobbler was the only one that remained calm. Standing on a chair amid the havoc, he sang his own tune.

'Bitterness is finally bidding goodbye
while a river is indeed beholding joy.'

SEVENTEEN

The golden sand was flirting playfully with the shoes of the two companions while the sun was quenching its rays with the light emanating from their reunion.

'The desert seems to become less vast with the right company,' Quirky ascertained.

'But at the same time, the people become more dependent,' Cynic added.

'The usual doubts are plaguing your mind. I think it is about time for you to put them aside.'

'If you repeat a story to yourself for too long, you end up believing it. Then you get trapped in its claws, confirming it over and over again almost compulsively.'

'So we are the stories that we narrate to ourselves.'

'Definitely.'

'Let's intervene and change their flow, then. Let's agree that the old pen is out of ink,' she urged him.

'Yet we still hold the pen tightly in our hands. We are afraid.'

'If we put it down, we will kick away our past. And that torturing story is what has actually established us as narrators. Isn't that what you are getting at?'

'Do we dare tear up our identities into small pieces? Do we dare strip ourselves of the cloak of the omniscient narrator and invade destiny as heroes? That has always been the most sacred question,' the young man said solemnly.

'Who can scorn the honors given to the hero?'

'Heroes fall even before they rise, and we have always associated the fall with death itself. We, therefore, seek a functional interval. Neither ecstasy nor despair. Half-open arms and, as a result, a somewhat smaller crash at the end of the performance.'

'You have indeed crossed the river,' Quirky declared.

'I have seen. I know. I have always known. We all know. Yet we are reluctant to break the fetters and part with ways that are simultaneously familiar and grim.'

'Vicious cycle.'

'Wrong cycle.'

'It is likely that we met for a serious reason,' the artist mumbled.

'I can't rule that out.'

'Have I changed a great deal?' she wanted to know.

'You have aged,' he teased her.

'You are exaggerating. I am still quite a few years away from degeneration,' she rebutted.

'You will, however, get old. Someday. Not very far from today. Time aims at our youth, claiming speed medals.'

'Some verses are dancing in my mind:
"The present renders you immortal
if you let go of the redundant."'

'Let's drink some water to that, then. To the present that allows us to dream and to the future that may prove to be merciful with us.' The young man toasted.

'Let's drink to all the revolutions that have allowed us not to die from boredom,' she counter proposed.

A white fence soon appeared in front of the two old friends, like a white canvas that sought masterly brushes. And then the green oasis, a nature that bid winters goodbye, wearing its festive clothes.

'Oh, what wings will you be granted

if in the depth of your heart,

the spring you manage to keep shielded?' the mysterious door asked.

Cynic took Quirky by the arm, and they passed through the door into the new world. The pages of their story, the only one that they allowed themselves to narrate, were abandoning the dusty books while the riddles were racing toward their solutions.

'We are omniscient narrators before we become the protagonists of our story,' the young man revealed.

'We did set out for the broken pieces. Anyway, we always set out on a journey for such things,' the girl responded.

The sun's rays were scorching the unexplored land. The heat was unbearable, so the people were wandering around highways and alleyways in bathing suits. They all had a big smile on their face, so permanent that it seemed like a tattoo, and a rousing melody was coming out of what you could swear were the loudspeakers of the sky.

In that land, the summer seemed to last forever, and the passersby were exuding an unbridled happiness that deprived them of even the smallest sense of prudence. The cars were running like demons, but the pedestrians insisted on crossing the streets carelessly and relied on their good fairy to look after them.

Soon, a deafening noise drew the attention of the two fellow travelers. A red race car had seriously injured a middle-aged woman. She was lying unconscious on the ground, and the blood blurred her features. A crowd of people had gathered around her. The doctor who had rushed to give her medical assistance was frantically taking her pulse.

'Her condition is critical. Of course, optimism is of paramount importance here,' he deliberated.

'She will be as good as new if we really believe it,' the people were saying among themselves.

The ambulance soon came, and two cheerful men, who were exchanging jokes with each other, carried the victim off on a stretcher.

Cynic and Quirky were shocked.

'The poor woman is fighting for her life, and they just go on as if nothing has happened.' The young man was annoyed.

The crowd soon dispersed in different directions and continued to walk with their eyes in the sky and their feet in the clouds.

The two old friends resumed their walk through the strange land with its bright colors, wild parties, and burning sun.

'I see a pastry shop at the corner. It looks tempting. Let's have a rest and get something to sweeten our palates there,' the artist suggested.

'Okay,' Cynic halfheartedly agreed.

A waitress welcomed them. She was dressed in shocking pink from head to toe.

'What a wonderful day we are having today!' she exclaimed.

'A human life may have been lost in front of our very eyes just a few minutes ago, but the sun is still shining, and the birds are chirping away. I suppose this is what is of utmost importance in your world,' the young man replied.

'The woman will live,' the waitress answered with confidence.

'Of course! And she will soon take out her favorite swimsuit from her closet and wear it,' Cynic commented with sarcasm.

'Exactly! What would you like to order? We have so many delicious treats here that I really don't know what to recommend. So many treats, such variety!'

'Some ice-cream for me. What flavors do you have?' Quirky asked.

'Our refrigerators have not been working for quite a long time.'

'I bet you consider this a great piece of news,' Cynic said with a sigh.

'The problem will soon be taken care of. Or, rather, the challenge, not the problem. There are no problems.'

'I see. And how long have your refrigerators been revolting?' he insisted.

'Who counts time…?'

'Then, what can we actually order?'

'Only preserved fruit.'

'Fine. Bring us both preserved figs.'

'We are out of figs.'

'Bring whatever you wish. Anyway, whatever you have,' Quirky intervened.

'Bitter orange.'

'Bitter orange it is, then.' The two friends agreed.

'Superb!'

'Fantastic!'

The waitress left.

At the next table, a red-haired young woman was reading her newspaper carefully.

Once in a while, she circled some things with a pencil. Every now and then she exclaimed, 'Great news!' or 'Very promising!'

'That girl reminds me of someone,' the artist mumbled.

'She is holding a trashy tabloid, and she is enthusiastic about everything it says as if she, playing the role of Alice, is exploring the ink of wonders.'

'She could just be reading the latest news.'

'I can already visualize the headline: "Middle-aged woman is dying, but she will wake up from the coma with the help of positive thinking."'

'Let's not exaggerate—'

'Everything around us constitutes an exaggeration,' Cynic argued.

'I will talk to her,' the artist decided and boldly approached her at once.

'Good morning.'

'Hi. I haven't seen you around here before, right?' the stranger answered.

'Right. We have set off on an adventure, and this land is a brief stopover in our long journey. What are you reading, if I may ask?' The adopted daughter of the most perfect of the perfect ones was curious.

'I have studied anthropology, and sometimes I like to check the ads that pertain to this field.'

'They must be teeming with work opportunities in this area.'

'Actually, there are not many openings for work in my field. The openings involve positions that will be available in the next decade. I have already noted five such posts. Extremely significant. For my qualifications, anyway.'

'If there are no prospects, why don't you seek your future elsewhere?' Cynic got into the conversation.

'Excellent question, but I have put a lot of effort and passion into my laboratory. Besides, I have a unique—almost metaphysical—hope that ills can be corrected with profuse optimism and tenacity,' the red-haired girl countered.

'You love your science, so you refuse to give up,' Quirky concluded.

'I avoid mechanical work, and I breathe freely only when I am being creative,' the stranger agreed.

'But how do you make ends meet financially?' Cynic brought her down to earth.

'I do odd jobs here and there until the right moment, and I have our appointment. Or, rather, until the right opening for a job appears.'

'I wouldn't call your plans realistic.'

'I know you have a long way ahead of you, but I am tempted to invite you to my laboratory. I have a rich collection of skeletons from various historical periods, and I am as proud of them as a mother is of her children.' The anthropologist changed the subject.

Quirky looked at her friend, seeking his consent. He nodded in agreement.

'We will not decline your kind invitation. We are struggling to solve the mystery of life, but, who knows, it may be wiser once in a while to start at the end,' the artist commented.

'Great! I apologize for not introducing myself all this time, but I have a problem with names. Would you mind if we stayed away from banalities?'

'We feel the same way,' the two friends noted.

The stranger's laboratory was situated just a few blocks away from the pastry shop. It was a sparkling-clean basement in excellent condition. The low light gave it a mystical charm. The two old classmates removed their shoes and entered hesitantly.

For a few minutes, they stared around and seemed to be at a loss.

'I do hope that my subject matter does not make you tremble with fear. I will, of course, respect your fear. Mortals are afraid of the end, and I, shamelessly, pit them against darkness.'

'Skeletons can be counted as a problem. Sorry, I meant as a challenge. Very well kept, I must say,' Cynic pointed out and, at the same time, hoped that the army of skulls that was staring at him from a corner would not attack him.

'Oh, I am so glad you noticed that. I polish them all the time, you know.'

'For the five positions that may or may not be proclaimed in a decade,' he guessed.

'I will be prepared.'

'When was it that you realized that you were born for this particular work?' Quirky asked curiously.

'Our mission always calls upon us. We, of course, often whistle indifferently, fearing the frustrations that the journey to ecstasy may be hiding,' the girl answered.

'Did you grow up here?'

'I usually avoid talking about my beginnings. You see, I keep deep inside me a huge cloud of bitterness. Yet today, I yearn for those beginnings, so if you want to find out where I grew up, I have something to show you,' she said while she was groping deep inside a huge box, arousing their curiosity. 'I found it. For the rest of the people, this is nothing but a simple drawing. For me, however, it is a magnificent world that was unfairly shattered,' she informed them and showed them the paper.

Its surface suddenly brought to life a crowd of people who were singing, writing, playing, and staying immortal. In their midst, a swaggering man seemed to coordinate their actions just like a bandleader. It was a long-gone era. It was the Castle of Divergence.

Quirky and Cynical were speechless. The young woman immediately felt their tension and got the distinct feeling that a new day was dawning.

' "To my friend, Optimist, who has been endowed with many talents and sees beauty everywhere." Isn't that what the dedication says?' the judge's adopted daughter managed to mutter.

The scientist's eyes kept going from one young person to the other while her body remained motionless. Cynic approached her, and so did the artist. The three youths were now joining hands and looked like proud trees that were getting rid of their bareness. *Ring-a-round the rosie, A pocket full of posies, Ashes! Ashes! We all fall down.* Childhood memories that refused to die away.

'To the castle pieces that will eventually unite our hearts,' Optimist exclaimed tearfully.

'To *someday* that has become *now*,' Quirky added. 'Optimist, there is a river somewhere at the end of the country, isn't there?' she asked a few minutes later.

'Yes, and there is a boatman there that takes people across,' the scientist said indifferently.

'Haven't you ever crossed the river?'

'I have never had the time.'

'I think you should take the journey with us now,' her friend said in a low voice.

'I would love to do so, but I find it impossible to abandon my work,' the scientist mumbled.

'You deserve both a break and an opportunity,' Cynic insisted.

Before long, Optimist decided to give in to her friends' exhortations.

***

The three of them were walking and chatting happily until they made out the river in the distance. The same mysterious boatman helped them board his 'famous' boat and later bid them goodbye with the familiar wink and a slightly wider smile.

On the other bank of the river, the weather exuded sweetness. The people there seemed content and carefree; nonetheless, just to be safe, they did take a look left and right before they crossed the intersections.

Gathered in a circle around a fountain, a group of teenagers were talking about the famous scientist who, shut up in his laboratory for decades, made great discoveries and saved many people from terminal illnesses. They professed their desire to be like him when they grew up. At present, however, they had ample time, so they ended their discussion quickly, got on their roller skates, and glided along the highway of their youth, where there is always an awful lot of time and countless prospects.

Cynic grabbed the newspaper that the students had trampled over on the ground.

'Mr. Petrakos provides hope and smiles,' the headline read.

After asking the local people for information, the three friends found out that Mr. Petrakos' laboratory was one kilometer away, so they set out impatiently to meet him.

They rang his doorbell hesitantly. Soon, an elderly man let them in. He was wearing a white robe which seemed to be in perfect harmony with his completely white hair. The sweat that was trickling down his face had steamed up his small glasses.

Despite his apparent exhaustion, he welcomed the three strangers eagerly. Oddly enough, he did not ask for any explanations.

'Travelers do pay me a visit once in a while, so I am not surprised by your presence here. Besides, I love this sort of interaction. I have a lot of hard work ahead of me, but I will gladly take some time off for your sake. Come to my little sitting room and make yourselves at home. I will serve you savory tea, the perfect fuel for troubled hearts,' he told them gently.

'We don't want to put you to any trouble,' Quirky interrupted him.

'It is my pleasure!' he replied cheerfully. He returned a few minutes later, holding a tray.

'I am listening. I suppose a serious reason has brought you to my place.' Mr. Petrakos broke the awkward silence.

Cynic got straight to the subject. 'This young lady here claims to be a scientist and lives on the other bank of the river.'

'The truth is that in the place where I previously resided, scientists were not treated with respect,' the elderly researcher answered.

'Are we fellow countrymen?' Optimist was surprised. 'We are still facing the same challenges there,' she confided in him.

'She means problems.' Cynic rushed to clarify.

'I have always believed that optimism is an inherent quality of enlightened souls. However, when it ends up as a complete utopia, it proves to be extremely dangerous. I am carrying a lot of years on my back and quite a few experiences too. If there is one thing I have learned from my course in life, it is that I should avoid chimeras.'

'Difficulties do not demoralize me. And, believe me, that is all I face,' Optimist answered with tears in her eyes.

'You have made up your mind to achieve your goal no matter what happens, so I am sure you will do so. However, let go of the futile struggles and concentrate only on the sublime ones. I cannot read the future, but I find it perfunctory to rely only on fate. And something else. You should just regard your heart as your true and permanent homeland.'

Optimist finally understood. Even more importantly, this understanding made her fully aware that there was no turning back.

As soon as they finished their tea, the three friends bid their kind host goodbye.

'Are we all leaving together?' Cynic asked.

'Let's not pressure her,' Quirky suggested.

'To the broken pieces that will unite our hearts once again,' the anthropologist shouted.

The three of them were now swimming together in the seas of destiny, just like all the friends who unearth boats in the abyss and draw rainbows in the middle of stormy oceans.

***

The waves reached a crescendo, craving for the prevalence of justice, while in the Castle of Perfection, the foundations were once again shaking with rage. The photographer crawled under a sturdy table and held his breath while the distinguished surgeon was running around frantically.

The earthquake lasted quite a few seconds this time. When it was over, Judge Compulsion came out of his hiding place feeling humiliated, and a new word smiled at him with audacity from the once blank canvas: 'Hope.'

The judge went back to his hiding place in desperation.

EIGHTEEN

The three friends were moving on, but they were no longer in a hurry. In fact, every so often, they would stop for a few minutes as if they desperately desired to listen to the secrets of the wind. The secrets, that is, of the wind that dances between continents and oceans without sacrificing its free-spirited gust at altars.

The flowers were now blooming in the center of the oasis, just like a sunbeam that had long been awaiting its signal to appear. Truth be told, we are always in search of spiritual fertilizer and firm roots in our lives.

Optimist seemed exhausted from the journey, but she had full confidence in her fellow travelers. For years, she had been convinced that they would one day meet again, but the days passed, and the pain of absence wounded all her summers and winters. Separated for a short while had surrendered to separate for a long while, and the fear of eternal separation had loomed before her as a terrifying possibility.

'Well, it is either now or never,' Cynic shouted excitedly. It was true that anticipation was coming to an end, and the present was being tested against fears and dreams, light and darkness.

A tall, thin, dark-skinned man in white clothes was standing in front of the white fence. In his hands, he was carrying a basket full of compasses.

'How much do they cost?' the scientist asked him, thinking that such a device would prove to be very helpful in their long journey.

He checked out the travelers for quite a while.

'In the desert, we get lost only with our consent, so there is no need for compasses. We build them ourselves, and we make the people we love the compass hands,' he told them.

Then, he took a bow, grew huge wings and, like a butterfly, disappeared into the vast sky. The basket, along with its contents, mysteriously vanished as well. In its place, there were many humble caterpillars waiting patiently for their turn to fly high into the sky.

The green door was insistently asking the three friends: 'What is it that actually drives society to the sacred change?'

When the green door opened up, the old classmates beheld a new land. The autumn scenery was scattering many leaves to their feet, while the clouds turned into a gray cloak that shrouded the hazy landscape. The people were vacillating between opening and closing umbrellas, and the rain, an invisible threat, was menacing their dry clothes.

'Shortly before the outbreak,' Cynic commented.

However, it was still early; they had not seen anything yet.

In this land, neat, decent people were taking care of their nicely set up shops, and well-mannered men and women were wandering in the narrow streets with feeble voices and uncertain steps. Everyone seemed to either be going somewhere or feel the need to be going somewhere. Time was setting up a race, and the people seemed to be following out of breath. They were getting older. They were getting old. They eventually let out their final breath and had their watches covered with ample soil.

Outside the picturesque church of the square, a young man in a blue suit hesitantly approached the three friends.

'This gadget has broken down for good. Can you tell me what time it is?' he said, pointing at his watch.

'It is exactly twelve,' Quirky replied.

'I see. Late again.'

'I suppose you have a business appointment,' the artist surmised.

'Some kind of appointment,' he mumbled.

'Obviously with a girl. Don't worry, women are always late,' Optimist assured him.

'With a boatman,' the stranger corrected her.

'Do you wish to cross the river?'

'Yes. I wait for him every day at noon.'

'But he doesn't come,' the artist noted.

'I light candles. I pray.'

'Candles were not actually created to bestow favors. We often forget that, don't we?' Cynic pointed out.

'Who are you? I have never seen you before. We all know each other here quite well. In fact, you could say that we know both the good and the bad side of everyone,' the stranger wondered, and the indifference in his voice did not match at all his nervous movements.

'Do you guys have a bad side too? I am surprised. You seem to be people of proper behavior.'

'There is always a bad side. Don't fool yourself,' the young man answered gloomily.

'Do you lack courage?'

'Exactly. We have been born compliant. Soldiers that carry out their duties perfectly. So the mechanism functions.'

'It functions, but it does not redeem,' the anthropologist remarked.

'And you wish to escape from your world,' Cynic concluded.

'I am trying... ' the stranger said, lowering his head.

'You considered the boatman your accomplice. He vowed to take you to the promised land.' Cynic continued his guesses.

'He doesn't speak. I insistently ask him if he will help, and he just nods. I take that to mean yes.'

'We eternally see in others what we want to see,' Quirky commented.

'Possibly,' the hostage of time muttered, disappointed.

'Why don't you set out to meet him?' Cynic asked.

'I need some encouragement.' The stranger excused himself and checked them over for a few minutes.

'You light candles to find this encouragement instead of getting on your feet.' Cynic now criticized him.

'Don't mind him. He is a bit blunt.' Optimist excused her friend.

'I used to know someone like him. Let me just take the chance to tell you a story. You know, I have squeezed so many valuable memories into this umbrella that I pointlessly carry with me at all times,' the stranger said, fumbling in its casing. He soon brought out the broken piece of the miniature of the castle.

'You probably think I am crazy not to have gotten rid of this broken piece,' he continued, and his eyes got watery.

The old friends were on tenterhooks.

'I know it is you. I have been waiting for you. I have been dreaming about you at night, and I have been anticipating our escape,' he said before they could utter a word.

'But how?' The travelers were shocked.

'I remember you always saying that I am a person of few words. I didn't talk a lot, but I did observe every little detail about you. And it was the small details that led me back to our common past.'

Then they held each other's hands in the familiar circle of the past, the circle that contained the memories in the schoolyards and bound their destinies in books.

'Do you think that you will stand up the boatman if you get up and leave now?' the artist said, as the tears were trickling down her face.

'He deserves to be stood up,' he answered, smiling.

They moved on once again. All of them this time. The four broken pieces of a childhood that could never be brought back, but also the four broken pieces of a love that had not faded in the least. Reserved started telling his old friends all about his country.

'As I have already mentioned, everything here goes according to plan,' he started.

'Except for your watch, of course, which has gone crazy,' the judge's adopted daughter said in jest.

'It has been showing the wrong time for quite a while. What is really strange is that I had it repaired many times, but as soon as I got outside the church, it always broke down again.'

'Hm… it is as if it advises you not to just sit around and wait for the right moment,' Optimist commented.

'To create it yourself,' Cynic added.

'Perhaps. Let me not be misunderstood. Decent people reside in my land. However, the days come and go, and they are always identical. In the same office and house, the same stagnant marriage, the same boring company, and the same disciplined agendas. That is, they come and go in a routine that kills us little by little.'

'You don't dare to express yourselves. Yet we eternally face situations that flare up our fears,' the scientist noted.

'Until we conquer them. Somewhere deep inside, you found the courage. That's why your watch broke down, and that is also why we appeared before you,' Cynic added.

'In the last two years, I have been feeling restless. And then, the sleepless dawns questioned the bed of complacency,' Reserved confessed.

'The boatman!' Cynic exclaimed.

'He wasn't going to come,' the artist declared.

'He was waiting for me,' the hostage of watches said.

'He was waiting for you,' the anthropologist agreed.

Soon, the four friends got on the boat and, a little while later, had crossed over to the other bank of the river. The boatman suddenly broke his silence.

'It was a pleasure to be with you. We did not exchange a single word, but we did share a ride. The most sacred one. You carry a great deal of madness in those heads of yours; otherwise, you would not have ended up here. You will break the curse. I can feel it. Every nod of mine has actually been a way to adorn your hearts with wings.'

'It is the *goodbye*,' Quirky said tearfully.

'There are no goodbyes, my dear. Only vicious cycles that we desperately draw until we remove them with the eraser of faith,' the boatman encouraged her.

The wanderers left behind that silent and mysterious man, the eternal transition from darkness to light, from habit to truth.

On the other bank of the river, the four friends were surprised by the heavy shower. The water came upon them and wet their clothes right through. Reserved fell to the ground and broke into sobs—disconsolate ones just like the storm that fused the dawn with the dusk. The raindrops were falling alongside the tears over all the bitterness that had been locked in the heart, over the laughter that had drowned in guilt, over the inhibitions that had not been showered with gratitude.

Yes, it was truly the opposite bank of the river. It was the clouds that were conquering the outburst, and it was the watches that were carrying out the escape from the labyrinth.

***

On the other side of the world, a drop from the heavy storm had mysteriously broken into Compulsion's apartment. For a while, it tickled his forehead and wet his crooked mouth. Then it took on the colors of the rainbow, only to finally land proudly on the once blank canvas that was slowly acquiring life.

'Courage,' it wrote.

The judge grabbed the sponge, soaked it in alcohol, and attempted in desperation to wipe out the letters. An exercise in futility. Sublime ideas become words, and these words never die.

NINETEEN

There was no longer desert land, just small slides that led to a bigger one, which was attired in each and every color available on Earth. Our heroes descended the slides with great speed while the old worlds fused right before their eyes. Who they had been and who they were going to be breathed in the same body, the same journey that turned the universe upside down.

Eventually, the friends landed in a room that looked like a living room. They could see four doors on their left and on their right. The only other thing in the room was a bar further inside. Behind the counter, an attractive man was mixing cocktails and smiling in their direction.

'Hey, you! Come over here. No human soul has come this way for quite a long time,' he called out to them.

The friends approached the stranger hesitantly. The screens in the background were monitoring some people with backpacks exploring every corner of the planet.

'So, you are both a barman and a spy,' Cynic noted.

'Explorer, just like you. My name is Phoebus.' He introduced himself. 'Just before the curtain falls, I try to ease your tension with alcohol.'

'You are speaking as if we are taking part in a theatrical play,' Optimist said in surprise.

'Everything is like partaking in a play of sorts. Or, at least, it should be. If we get rid of the dust in our souls, then perhaps we can be reborn.'

'Until then, let's have some wine,' Cynic suggested.

'The finest! For the brave and outstanding ones. For those who salvage hopes.'

'You must be waiting for something here,' Reserved pointed out.

'I have wandered around a great deal. You see, from a very young age, I refused to accept confining borders and strict limitations. However, it is impossible for me alone to carry on my back the new age. I have been looking for company to share the burden. The right company. Very few travelers have got to the end of the journey, and those who have managed to reach it failed in this last challenge.'

'And then?' Quirky asked, quite shaken by his words.

'They wander from place to place seeking something, yet they never manage to find it,' the barman answered, pointing at the monitors. They are consumed by the sense of the unfulfilled, the insatiable. They grow old with this grief. They did see. However, they saw through a half-closed door which they, unfortunately, never managed to open up completely. They are trapped in the interspace, and they are balancing on the tightrope that distinguishes insight from illusion.

'Why don't they just cut the rope?' Cynic wondered.

'There is no rope, my friend. Our mind creates the ropes.'

'It seems that you have been a witness to many failures. Perhaps we will manage to overcome the difficulties with your assistance,' Optimist said.

'You will run up against your worst fears. In such duels, we are always alone,' the barman explained.

'I was under the impression that we had already conquered our fears,' the artist objected.

'They always come back at the last minute. They test our stamina and begrudge more than anything else the steel of happiness.'

'Let the procedure begin. We hereby declare ourselves ready,' Cynic stated.

'Very well! You can see the doors on the two sides of the shop. As you can see, they are numbered from one to four. You decide which one of them each of you will open. Nonetheless, whichever one you open will be indisputably your door.'

'Let's open them up in the order that we met each other,' Reserved suggested.

'So, I start,' Quirky shouted boldly.

'Good luck! Remember one thing: the tightrope does not exist; it has never existed,' Phoebus reminded her.

The girl pushed the door resolutely, and a long black corridor welcomed her. She walked on it for quite a few minutes until it led her to a fabulous art exhibition. The countless heads of the elegant guests were hiding the works of art. A piano player at the far end of the room was caressing the piano keys with his fingers, and every caress was spinning out another imposing note. He was wearing a white suit, and his upright figure revealed his aristocratic background.

The young woman approached him and touched him lightly on the shoulder. Immediately, a trapdoor opened up, right in the center of the room. It drew inside it all the art lovers. The pianist turned his face to the girl, and she screamed with fear. The work of art that had brought about her escape from the judge's kingdom was now smiling at her in a melancholy way from every inch of the room, and it seemed to be whispering to her that we never really get rid of our fears; we do not exorcise the gray, and we do not shed light on the annoying shadows.

'What comes around goes around, my dear.' Compulsion was laughing hysterically.

'Please… let me go,' she mumbled.

'Destroy your work of art immediately! If you do so, the reputation of the Castle will be restored, and time will go back to the moment that the gates opened to welcome the mediocre people. Your name will be heard again, but this time you will not come forth to denounce the sacred vision of the perfect society. And then everything will go back to the way it was. Everything will be back to normal!' he repeated loudly.

'I refuse to surrender to your wishes,' the young woman muttered. 'The *before* was my prison, and I will not go back to my prison cell.'

Then, the man put his strong arms around her neck. Her breaths came out trembling, and the sense of suffocation came back from its lethargy and was taking away her life little by little. Phoebus and her friends were anxiously watching her on the monitor.

'She has turned pale.'

'It is as if she is fighting with someone.'

'She is suffering. Let's run to her.'

'Impossible. It is her battle; it is her life,' the barman pointed out.

Quirky finally managed to take a deep breath and immediately recovered her self-control. She looked at the judge straight in the eye.

'I am safe. I have no dealings with shadows any longer. Other people's hands no longer deprive me of my oxygen,' she burst out.

The distinguished judge fell into the trapdoor at once, and a dove was drawn right in the center of the painting. A door opened wide, and the artist returned to the broken pieces of a heart that scorned its oppressors.

Phoebus was looking at her with his eyes full of tears. 'You destroyed the tightrope.'

'You were right. It was just an illusion.'

'At one time, you were given the name Acrobat. We all cover our stories with identity cards,' he told her gently. 'Yet, we have a long way ahead of us before we can make those identity cards a reality. The rest of the doors remain closed and deprive us of the ability to see the new society,' Phoebus continued. 'I believe it is your turn.' He turned to Cynic, who continued sipping his wine.

'Don't you feel ready?' Reserved asked him apprehensively.

'I would prefer to go in last so that I may enjoy my drink. If you don't mind, of course,' he answered, trying to sound indifferent.

'You have become agitated,' Phoebus noted.

'I just wish for some more time. Let's not make a big deal of it,' he answered in the same indifferent tone.

'I will go in his place,' Optimist said courageously.

'I will choose the third door since, let's not forget, I was the third traveler that joined this group,' she announced cheerfully to everyone.

She then walked along the long black corridor until she saw a high-class restaurant ahead. A man was standing at the entrance.

'We are famous for our spoon sweets,' he informed the scientist, and this reminded her of her previous homeland, where every proper host served his guests a particular spoon sweet, bitter orange.

The restaurant was empty, which surprised the young woman, but she figured that maybe it was too late and the customers had gone back to their homes and to their loved ones who were waiting for them.

Optimist made herself comfortable at one of the tables in the center of the restaurant and, as soon as she did so, she felt that the place was suddenly teeming with satisfied faces, sated looks, and warm voices. Soon, a woman approached her. She was carrying a tray, but instead of serving delicious delicacies, she served a newspaper.

'Do you remember me?' she asked the scientist.

'Certainly. You served us at the pastry shop where I met my friends.'

'That's right. I have been working here for a decade. The heating is evidently not working, and the refrigerators present many challenges, but the Gordian knots can be solved in good spirit. Don't you agree?'

'Naturally! Optimism disarms the knots. I apologize for my uneasiness, yet—I won't hide this from you—I am surprised to meet you in this place. Are you also finishing your journey?'

'You must be kidding. I amble around the earthly paradise every single day and, consequently, have no particular curiosity regarding the rest of the world. However, I am here to serve you exciting news.'

'I am listening,' Optimist said, bursting with curiosity.

'If my memory does not deceive me, you were looking through the ads for work openings back in our country.'

'I was checking the newspaper on a daily basis.'

'Look at the last page of the newspaper. It says it clearly. There will be a job opening in your field in five years.'

The scientist spontaneously got up and kissed the woman on both cheeks.

'Five years. It is not such a long time. My money is running out, but I will think up a solution to my financial problem.'

'Actually, we need help at the shop, so you are hired. Shall we go back home, then?' The woman put out her hand.

Optimist felt her legs heavy with hesitation. She'd had quite a hard time paying the rent for some months. Five years had a lot of months on their back. With reason as her shield, she remained still.

'Don't think of throwing away such an opportunity,' the waitress sternly warned her.

'Go away!' the scientist shouted at her in a decisive manner.

At that moment, the newspaper came to life and wrapped the waitress inside its pages. The ink turned into a black sea, and it carried her into the depths of its dark waters. Then the newspaper took on its normal form and landed with force in the anthropologist's hands. The job opening had disappeared from its last page. In its place, there was a sentence in golden letters: 'Our heart is our homeland.'

Optimist, quite content, started on her way back.

'It is happening. It is truly happening,' Phoebus was saying to himself, really touched by what he had seen.

Reserved got ready, as it was his turn to summon his destiny.

He opened the fourth door, and his feet slowly moved down the long black corridor. He eventually saw a theatrical stage ahead. There were about twenty people sitting in the comfortable chairs set out for the audience. A young woman was running her hands through her thick hair, and a middle-aged man in a suit was biting his lips nervously. They all seemed to be waiting for something.

The traveler sat next to a pretty, dark woman with honey-colored eyes. She was wearing a blue dress.

'Hi, there.' She greeted him, allaying his anxiousness. 'How did you find out about the magic genie?'

The young man was baffled. However, before he had time to answer, the infamous genie appeared on the stage. It was extremely big, with slanting black eyes and long red hair tied at the back of its head.

'Ladies and gentlemen, I am standing here in front of you tonight to remind you that, on nights like this, the skies open up and make our wishes a reality,' the mysterious creature claimed.

Then he fixed his gaze on Reserved.

'Come!' it told him.

Reserved was surprised, as he had never had any confidence in his good luck. Blushing with embarrassment, he went onto the stage and stood facing the genie.

'You know quite well who I am and what I can do for you. In fact, my reputation has traveled all over the world for centuries. It is now your turn to be granted three wishes. Think of them swiftly because my oil lamp does not forgive procrastinators.'

Reserved withdrew to a corner and was deep in thought regarding desires and doubts. The audience gradually became annoyed over his taking far too long to decide.

'Why doesn't he decide what he wants?' someone muttered.

'Or let me take his place,' someone else said.

'Choose me,' the woman in the blue dress called out.

Reserved was now certain that his first wish would involve love and specifically the woman in the blue dress. However, before he could utter a word, a man put his arms around her in an aggressive manner.

'She is mine.' He made it quite clear.

'My friend, do not pay attention to him. You set up the rules of this performance,' the genie reminded him. 'But you must decide right away, as there are far too many dreams for me to save,' he warned.

Reserved wished to say his desire out loud, but, for some strange reason, his voice would not come out.

'Speak,' the audience urged him.

'Believe in us,' the woman pleaded with him.

Suddenly, the genie withdrew despondently to his lamp. He took the audience with him, as well as their numbered seats. The room was covered wall to wall with thousands of watches instead of rugs. The man who had just deprived him of a wish and a love was now standing right in front of Reserved. He was dressed in gray from head to toe. He had black hair, a pointed chin, huge limbs, and sharp nails. In his hands, he held an hourglass.

'Where are you off to, my friend?' he asked, and his abrasive voice was painful to the ears.

'I am completing my fateful exploration,' Reserved replied hesitantly.

'Nonsense. You will return, with your tail between your legs to your previous life, to the land of inactivity and to rain that never comes,' the stranger said sarcastically. 'You see, you have wasted a great opportunity. That is exactly why you are trapped in a place where time moves backward,' he continued while Reserved felt his pulse rising.

'Except... except if you break all the watches within the deadline,' he suddenly shouted.

'But there are thousands of them,' the young man mumbled.

'That is exactly why it will be fun for me to watch,' the man said and turned the hourglass upside down.

Reserved grabbed the watches in his hands; he bit some with all his might and others he crushed with his two legs. However, they all kept going back to their previous state, causing him great despair.

At some point, as if he woke up from lethargy, he gave up his struggle and stood still and calm in his place.

'You do not exist. *Nothing* can have power over me, and time, like a good friend, reminds me that a fabulous life is awaiting me to enjoy it,' he shouted bravely at the stranger.

The man at once turned to powder that got trapped in the hourglass. The long black corridor opened up and united the young man with his friends, who embraced him warmly.

'I am the only one left,' Cynic noted.

Phoebus was watching him, deep in thought.

'Hell, just come out and say it,' he urged the young man. 'It will prove far more difficult for you than you can even imagine. Before you toss the coin, take a good look behind you, perhaps the look that signals a *goodbye*.'

'Message received. Relax, brother. You have been stuck in this place far too long, and it seems to me that you are tired of drinking all alone. I do understand how you feel, but I, for one, cannot stand pressure. My temperament just cannot put up with pressure of any sort. How can I make you understand this?' Cynic was furious.

'Don't throw the broken pieces into the vast ocean,' Phoebus implored him.

Cynic stood up straight and, feigning indifference, opened the door that corresponded to his destiny. Immediately, a huge dark hole took him by surprise and sucked him violently to its bottom, where there was a small wooden room.

There was a fire in the fireplace, and a young woman was smugly pressing the keys of a typewriter. As soon as she heard the young man's footsteps, she got up from her seat and went toward him. Her white dress was caressing her ankles while the flames of the fire were burning in her gray eyes, bringing sad memories violently to the surface.

Cynic welled up as the figure from his past began to hum a familiar melody.

'Our song. Could it be that you have forgotten it?' she asked him, and her voice was dancing a desperate tango with all the loves that ended before their time.

'You are the one that forgot it. That is why you left,' he answered sharply, with his head down as if he were looking for something on the ground. It could be that he was looking for solid roots to finally build a home.

'There was no sense in it. We come and go constantly. "Whoever daydreams is a fool." Those were your words.'

'I was happy near you,' he whispered to her.

'I chose that happiness as a memory, instead of superficial kisses and yawns in bed.'

'What is this now? I don't give second chances, you know.' He made it clear to her.

'There are no such things. Only desires for the sake of which we turn the earth upside down. I have come to bring you to your senses.'

'I feel nothing but contempt for anyone who lectures.'

'You left your comfort zone, you reconsidered your hippy theories, and you have gotten close to people who frequent bars. We, however, know quite well that the illusions that are fed can swallow us like wild animals. Whoever touches the depth of our soul abandons us. They grow old and eventually die. You have always struggled with depression. "Closeness ends up in excruciating pain. Laugh and seduce bodies from a distance." This is what you used to say,' she reminded him.

'I have changed. I have understood. I have felt—after a very long time.'

'You sneak out of likes before they turn into love.'

'Not any more,' Cynic mumbled.

'You will weep. Whatever you have feared will persecute you. Awake at many a dawn, you sought to exorcise the futility of mortality. Carefree is he who does not assume responsibilities, and relationships mete out quite a few of them,' she told him without taking a breath.

'I abandon before I am abandoned. A miserable man who parades his cowardice as if it were a medal—that is what I am. I tremble at the idea of loss, and so I provoke it,' he realized with bitterness.

'I stand in front of you today with an opportunity. The opportunity for you to escape from what has wounded you deeply. This typewriter is considered magical. Don't ask me how I got it. I believe that whatever we seek with passion always comes our way. So, you push keys and erase painful emotions until, just like blank paper free from sloppy smudges, you can make a new start. You can be reborn in a world where your parents have not been killed, the director that is dying in his prison cell has never come into your life, your friends, who once scattered to the four corners of the horizon, have never existed, and I have never taken my hat and left to make my home in another tent because I have simply been a figment of your imagination.'

'But we carry in our souls the pieces of everyone we have loved,' Cynic muttered.

'Yet, you will no longer need anyone. You will finally feel free,' she whispered in his ear, gently caressing his hand.

'You are right. I have no other choice but to erase all the memories that are killing me.' He moved back, breathing heavily, and took his place in front of the magical device.

His past lover sat on his knees. However, seconds before his finger touched the first key, he felt Phoebus' voice visiting his mind. *Do not throw the broken pieces into the vast ocean.*

Cynic jumped up from the armchair and, in one move, turned the typewriter upside down.

'Don't be naïve.' His old lover tried to talk some sense into him.

He pushed her away violently. Then, the keys became giant claws and trapped the woman inside the magical gadget. Subsequently, they started moving rhythmically.

'People die of loneliness and not of love,' they wrote on the blank paper.

The young man started on his way back, but there was no corridor to cross. He was now passing through a giant circus where the acrobats fell off the tightropes, died, and were reborn.

Soon he met his fellow travelers. The five friends embraced each other and started dancing in a circle. The broken pieces saved at once the hopes of the world, and the stars were no longer hiding timidly behind the bloody moon.

***

At the same time, the other side of the planet was struggling with the worst earthquake in its history. Objects were thrown all over the Castle.

'Hold on tightly to the wall,' the judge commanded every so often.

The perfect ones were huffing and puffing, all heated up, and they were defending themselves with all their strength against nature's attack. Yet the more they resisted, the greater the rumbling and the shaking.

The photographer was the first one to give up. 'Whatever has not been made from strong material is doomed to collapse,' he shouted, and the force of his words affected the ideal professionals who followed suit. One after the other, they gave up trying to hold up the walls and stood in the middle of the wreck.

Judge Compulsion was watching them from the corner of his eye until, all of a sudden, he also raised his arms.

'Whatever has not been made from strong material is doomed to collapse,' he repeated.

Then the Castle of Perfection crumbled like sand in the living room of the five friends. The monitors shattered at once, and the lost travelers jumped out of them and threw their backpacks into the air. The drinks at the bar turned into colorful butterflies, which wandered everywhere without a care in the world.

The perfect ones, after they had gotten over their initial shock, recovered from the nightmare and met their loved ones. The much-loved director got rid of his cuffs, and the photographer captured the magic of nature with his lens. The mouth of Judge Compulsion straightened, and he welcomed happiness with tears of relief. The cobbler, joyful, carried around his merchandise of new shoes.

'There are no good and bad people

just people

who stifle their hearts with weights.

Twenty years ago, you chose to have me along

as the prison you could not endure for long,' he sang

The sand whirled wildly in the wind until, finally, it was put in a glass container to remind us of the cages that we ourselves create and the ones which we break and escape from.

***

This is where I bid you goodbye, my friends. The hourglass will not allow me more time. I must cross a river now. We have narrated a story together, so I no longer consider you a stranger. Until we meet again, then. We will have some wine too. Let us drink to the friends that discover secret boats and map out grand journeys. I will remember you. As I always remember the outstanding and authentic people, all those who bring light to basements and dare to climb up steep paths. There you were. Here I was. Together we wrote a book. Our book. And a melody set the chords of the guitar into play. Our song, then—this is what we will leave behind.

www.ingramcontent.com/pod-product-compliance
Lightning Source LLC
LaVergne TN
LVHW091555060526
838200LV00036B/856